Liminal

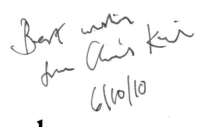

Best wishes
from Chris Keil
6/10/10

Liminal

Chris Keil

ALCEMI

First impression: 2007

Published with the financial support of the Welsh Books Council

Editor: Gwen Davies

ISBN: 9 780 95552 721 0
0 955 5272 1 X

Printed on acid-free and partly-recycled paper.
Published by Alcemi and printed and bound in Wales by
Y Lolfa Cyf., Talybont, Ceredigion SY24 5AP
e-mail ylolfa@ylolfa.com
website www.alcemi.eu
tel 01970 832 304

Chris Keil has run a sheep-farm, and has worked in journalism and as a teacher of English as a foreign language in a number of European countries. Recently returning to academic life and now lecturing worldwide, he has published on dissonant heritage and traumatic memory at Auschwitz. He lives in Carmarthenshire, west Wales, and currently lectures at Trinity College, Carmarthen. This is his second novel.

Prologue

She was walking so fast that they had to break into a skipping trot from time to time to keep up with her. On their left, the sea had turned milky, the line of stunted palm trees on the other side of the road silhouetted over the water. On the horizon, the lighthouse on the headland across the bay blinked palely. They were walking past a row of cafes and little restaurants, just opening up for the evening, a waiter in a white shirt setting out chairs on the pavement as a jangle of bouzouki notes followed them up the street. One bar was already busy; looking through the back into the kitchen, Geraint could see someone hefting a saucepan onto a dim blue flame. A boy in a red T-shirt clacked misted beer bottles onto a tray, scribbling the order on a pad and slipping the scrap of paper under a saucer of olives. There was a group of girls at an outside table: teenagers, elegant, darkly animated. One of them looked up with a flashing smile of recognition as they passed, and called out "Jessica!" The others joined in, waving and calling, their voices as sweet and mild as doves in the soft air: "Jessica! Jessica!"

She went over to their table and the girls fluttered round her, taking her hand, touching her hair, stroking the bright silk of her shirt. Musical phrases drifted over to Geraint and Angela, antiphonal trills of laughter. Angela blew her nose, and Jessica turned, pulling away from the girls, disengaging their hands.

"They're so sweet," she said as they set off again. She turned and waved at them. "They're so sweet."

"Who are they?" Angela asked.

"My students," Jessica said. "Some of them anyway. Aren't they lovely."

Geraint nodded, glancing back at them. They crossed a children's playground, passing between swings and climbing frames, their footsteps scuffing up cigarette-ends and puffs of dusty sand. A couple were sitting on a bench

7

under the shadow of the oleander bushes, cigarettes glowing and dimming in the twilight. A shallow flight of steps led up out of the playground onto a bigger street. Jessica turned and waited at the top for them. Angela missed her footing and stumbled for a moment.

"How far is this bloody place?" she said, raising her voice against the shrill buzz of a moped.

Jessica led them across the street, dodging between cars. A motor-bike, loaded with three kids clutching each other for balance, wobbled wildly past them. The narrow pavement was crowded with people, strolling, chatting, promenading with linked arms. Geraint and Angela walked in the gutter to move a little faster, trotting to keep up, stepping up into the press of bodies as cars pushed passed them, music thumping. He got separated from Angela, and stood waiting for her as people jostled past him. She reappeared, carried along in the crowd, her shoulders rounded. They stepped down into the road and hurried on.

Jessica was waiting for them outside a brightly lit café. They followed her into an area of tables looking out over the street, half covered over with a trellis of striped awnings and trailing plants, hung with lightbulbs. A middle aged woman appeared from the kitchen at the back and beamed at Jessica, taking her hand, patting her cheek, drawing the three of them over to a table.

"I came here a couple of times with Aled," Jessica said. "I thought maybe they could help us."

Angela's chair screeched across the tiled floor as she caught Geraint's eye.

"Plus the food's really good," Jessica said. There was a silence. A waiter shook out a paper table-cloth and wafted it down on the table, smoothing it and weighting it down with glasses, a jug of water, a basket of bread. He said something to Jessica, who nodded and smiled, gesturing with her hands. "Megalo," she said. "A big one." She smiled at Geraint. "We need some wine," she said. "Don't you think?"

From the bright terrace, framed in blue and white canvas, Geraint looked out onto the street, where ranks of strangers moved past in the evening light, like figures in a frieze.

"Last time you saw him," he began.

The waiter brought the wine in a dark earthenware jug. Jessica leaned across the table, filling their glasses.

"You saw him quite a bit then?" Angela asked her.

Jessica drank, shaking her head with an ambiguous gesture. "Sorry," she said. "Went down the wrong way. Good though, isn't it?" Geraint nodded, drinking again. He noticed Angela hadn't picked up her glass.

Jessica looked at her. "Not really," she said. "A few times." She took a piece of bread and pushed the basket across the table to them. The waiter set out plates, and a big oval dish of salad in the centre of the table. Angela blew her nose. The waiter gave her an admiring glance.

A couple settled themselves at the table next door, the man clicking his fingers for the waiter, setting out a packet of cigarettes and a lighter in front of him with fussy movements. He caught Geraint's eye and nodded, unsmiling. Jessica went into the kitchen to see what was happening with their food, coming back with another jug of wine. A second waiter came on duty as the place filled up, the level of noise seeming to rise in jerky increments, fragments of music glittering in the dark murmur of conversation, harsh notes of irritation or hilarity, sudden incomprehensible shouts, light and sound blurred through the smoke of cigarettes and grilling meat.

Geraint found himself looking over the top of his glass at Jessica; she was saying something to Angela, who nodded dolefully. Her name, he thought, was exactly right: Jessica…. He pursed his lips, afraid he'd been silently mouthing his thoughts, and set the wine glass down carefully in front of him.

Angela had been bundling about in her handbag, and now drew out a photograph mounted on a piece of card. Jessica took it, smiling as she angled it into the light.

"Not how I think of him at all," she said softly, her expression, it seemed to Geraint, inward and drowsy with memory.

"It's the best one I could find," Angela said sharply.

"Let me see it," Geraint said.

It was one of his graduation pictures, two years ago now. His gown hung lopsidedly as he posed, grinning, against the red brick of the college library. Geraint looked at the open, untroubled face, wide eyes that had nothing to do with mystery.

"It's good," he said, smiling back at the face in the photograph. "It's a good likeness."

Jessica had called the waiter over. He pulled up a chair and sat beside her, studying the photograph as she spoke to him, his eyes moving from her to Angela and back again.

"Anglos," Jessica was saying. "Anglos. English." She sighed. "My Greek

9

isn't up to this," she said.

"I thought you were a teacher," Angela said.

"I teach English," Jessica told her. "Not Greek."

She tapped the photograph. "Anglos," *she said again.* "Zeetoume afton ton andra. Prin apo theeo evthomathes. *Two weeks ago."*

She pointed to herself. "Me mena. With me."

The waiter nodded, his smile deepening.

"Wid you," he said. "Wid you." He looked up as a woman appeared in the doorway leading through to the back and called to him, her voice harsh as she gestured round at the crowded room. He motioned her over and she came to the table, nodding and smiling, wiping her hands on her apron before taking the photograph. "My mother," the waiter told them.

She handed the photograph back with a sudden cackle of laughter, wagging her finger at Jessica, shaking her head and chattering, her tone full of delighted disapproval.

"Two weeks ago," Jessica said again. "Prin apo theeo evthomathes." They both looked at her then, shrugging, heads tilted back and hands turned outward, before getting up from the table and walking back towards the kitchen. As they crossed the room, the old lady gave her son a shove and pretended to cuff him round the head. Geraint tipped the last of the wine into their glasses.

Part One

Separation

Chapter One

The waiting room was crowded. He sat down between an old couple, who shifted slightly to let him in. There was a set of shelves along the wall, divided into pigeon-holes full of leaflets, labelled by subject. *Alcoholism,* Geraint read, *Depression... Menopause... Anxiety.* He knew without looking that Mrs Evans was staring at him. The receptionist's phone rang and he caught Mrs Evans' eye. *Tinnitus... Constipation.* There'd been a run on that one, hardly any left. *Prostate.* Geraint sighed deeply. *Sexual problems.* He glanced through a magazine from the pile, stopping as a life-size nipple stared back at him from the glossy page, every detail in perfect focus. He flipped it shut and slid it back onto the pile. The old lady on his left eased herself a little further away. On the bench opposite, Mrs Evans glared at him. Geraint stared at his feet. The buzzer rang, and the girl behind the desk checked her screen; she called his name a little hesitantly, smiling.

Eleri sat him on a chair by her desk and gave him a curved pot to hold under his ear. "How's Aled?" she asked him. "Broken any more records yet?"

"I'm supposed to meet him at the track this afternoon." Geraint could sense her moving about behind him, but didn't like to look round to see what she was doing. She poked something into his ear, working it in until he coughed and screwed his eyes shut. A pump started up with a thin buzzing sound, and then a jet of icy water drummed in his ear.

"Alright?" she asked him. "Not too hot?"

He shook his head, wincing. The water sluiced inside his head. He shut his eyes again, imagining it scouring the canals of his skull, rushing through spirals and sockets of bone.

"*Duw, Duw,*" Eleri was saying. "Where's all this come from?"

The pump stopped buzzing. He could feel water trickling out of his ear and down his neck. Eleri shone a light in his ear.

"Better?" she said.

Geraint felt a bright gasp of sensation, as though a wind was blowing through his head.

In the car on the way to the track, he found himself thinking of the conversation he'd had with Lydia yesterday after the Friends of the Museum had left. He wondered whether she knew how he searched her face as they spoke. After their conversations he had only the vaguest sense of what had been said. He saw her lips, her teeth, the lucid face in front of him. He was distracted only when she made some extravagant gesture with her hands, long fingers raking the air. He had read her an extract from Giraldus Cambrensis, fetching the book down from the shelf, glancing at her as he read:

> "*A certain knight named Gilbert, after a long and unremitting anguish, which lasted three years, and the most severe pains as of a woman in labour, at length gave birth to a calf, an event which was witnessed by a great crowd of onlookers. Perhaps it was a portent of some unusual calamity yet to come. It was more probably a punishment exacted for some unnatural act of vice.*"

"Presumably," Lydia had murmured, smiling to herself, not looking at him, "involving a bull."

The traffic lights by the bridge seemed stuck on red. He laid his forehead against the warm glass of the window, looking out across a stubbly field. In the middle distance crows were circling round a little house. The windows were boarded up, and a tree had grown up through the chimney and then died, the whitened branches clawing stiffly against the sky, as though smoke had turned to bone.

On the other side of the river, the lower end of town was empty. The faraway roar of a military jet rose and fell, echoing, above him, as though there were fissures in the sky down which the sound ran, like mercury. The door of the White Swan was open onto the pavement, the dark interior cool. He turned left into the street that ran down towards the Leisure Centre. They hadn't collected the rubbish that morning; the multi-coloured garbage bags heaped outside front doors

13

along the street, had the look of the flowers that appear so quickly at scenes of death and tragedy.

The plastic bags reminded him of the latest donation, the contents of most of Protheroe's attic, by the look of it. The long table in the Conference Room was filled with bags and cardboard boxes. He'd unpacked a little of it: a record player, a gas fire, a couple of umbrellas; jars of pickled fruit from 1942, floating in khaki-coloured liquid like anatomical specimens; a set of fifty icing horns; a bag full of little tin dishes for baking madeleines. It would take a week to sort through it all.

At the running track, a breeze lifted the flag above the Pavilion, the dragon rippling, as though seen through water. The seats at the far end of the oval were mostly empty. A rattle of applause crossed the space as a race came to a desultory end, a group of runners breaking step over the line, as though some tight spring inside them had broken. He caught sight of Aled; the boy detached himself from the group and came towards him, pulling the numbered slip over his head and waving it.

"See that, Dad?" he called. "Lucky seven strikes again." He stooped and slipped off the running shoes, walking gingerly across on bare feet.

"Did I see what?" Geraint asked him.

Aled shook his head, smiling. "Angela's over there," he said. "Are we going for a drink?" He cupped his hands and shouted: "Hey Ange! You see that?"

They sat at a table by the plate glass wall of the bar, looking down through the well of the building into a basketball court where foreshortened figures bounced and boomed and echoed. Angela arranged the objects on the table between them, sliding an ashtray into the centre, and positioning salt and pepper on either side. Geraint found himself wondering again just what Aled saw in her, why he wanted to marry her. She was beautiful, of course, in a statuesque sort of way, but there was something conventional, over-controlled, about her. The phrase *carrying a torch* came into his mind. Angela was carrying a torch for Aled in exactly the way the Statue of Liberty carried a torch. She became aware of him watching her, and looked up with a short smile.

Aled brought drinks over. Geraint watched his son as the boy dipped his head to the pint glass, pursing foam off his lip. He had a sudden memory of an afternoon the two of them had spent blackberrying, the last day of the summer holidays. The fruit wasn't ripe, the taste as sharp as regret, but the intense sourness had been a challenge, making him grin, black-lipped.

"Then we thought: what about the Museum?" Angela was saying. "The big lawn at the front there, down to the pond. All those lovely trees. Wouldn't it be lovely? Mam thought so too."

She put her hand over Aled's, speaking for both of them. "We need lots of room after the church," she said. "We'll be going to the Holly Bush later, of course, the young people, I mean. But we thought: speeches, you know? And everybody gets a glass of champagne."

Geraint nodded. "What if it rains?" he said.

"Not if we had a marquee," Angela said. "Anyway, we need somewhere, long tables, to pour the champagne, you see. White tablecloths, flowers." She sighed, tightening her grip on Aled's hand. Over the rim of his glass, Aled rolled his eyes at Geraint, an ambivalent look.

"Sorry I missed the race," Geraint said.

"And it's having the car-park too," Angela said. "Not everywhere in town you can park a lot of cars."

Aled looked at his watch. "Better get back," he said. "Did Nana get hold of you?"

Geraint shook his head.

"She wants you to call round, something she wants to tell you."

At his mother's house, Geraint found the spare key under the flowerpot and let himself in. He stood in the dim hallway for a moment, breathing in the thin, characteristic odour: rubber, cabbage, and something sharper he could never quite define. He could hear voices from the kitchen. His mother got up as he came into the room.

"Just in time," she said. "Look who's here."

She had been sitting at the table with that little woman whose name he could never remember.

"Rosie," his mother said. "Back again, like the swallows. You

15

remember my son, don't you Rosie. She's been in North Wales, Rosie has. Sit down, Geraint, you're making me nervous, standing there."

"I was in Conwy," Rosie said. "A bit colder what I'm used to. Come along that A548 from Prestatyn. Busy road that."

Geraint watched her as she spoke. Must be about sixty, he thought. Her face had the grainy, reddened look of someone who lives outdoors, not very clean, but lit by an expression of extraordinary sweetness, bright and direct.

"Takes you through Rhyl," she was saying. "Won some award, that place; Most Boring Town in the world, or something." Her voice was curiously harsh and flat, distanced, as though she was reading. "Left it after Abergele," she said. "Took the B5381 after that, through Betws and Dolwen. Not much traffic; local, you know, farmers and that."

Geraint cleared his throat and looked at his mother. "You wanted to tell me something?" he said quietly, against the grain of Rosie's voice.

His mother widened her eyes at him. "Did I dear?" she said. "I don't think so."

"Course, you got to go to Conwy from there," Rosie said. "Unless you dropped down to Llanrwst. The A470 would get you there, but that can be busy. If it's wet you get that spray. There's a B-road, of course, B5113. You know that one?"

Geraint shook his head. "Aled told me," he said to his mother. "I saw him at the running track. He said you wanted to see me."

Rosie had been taking off various bits of clothes as she spoke: a scarf, a plastic rain-jacket. She had a long coat on under that, then a grey fleece; she slipped the coat off and hung it on the back of the chair. Geraint wondered where she slept at night on her travels, on her endless pointless pilgrimage to nowhere, an itinerary which never seemed to stop unrolling in her head.

His mother came to the front door with him. "You're always in such a hurry," she said. "It's like Aled, I never see him at all these days. And you're getting too thin."

"He told me you wanted to see me about something," Geraint said carefully.

"Not *about* something," his mother said. "Just to see you. I never

16

see you these days. Worse than Aled." She took his hand, patting it. "Do you think he's really going to marry that girl? She's too tall for him."

Geraint shrugged. "Looks like it," he said. "So there's nothing you need? You sure?"

She smiled at him. "I better get back to Rosie, I'm going to make her something to eat. Tell Aled to come and see me."

At the Museum, a couple of teenagers pushed prams slowly past the display of mesolithic arrowheads, turning to stare at stone axes and Bronze Age daggers. In his office, Geraint called Lydia's number, but there was no reply. He got out the file on the Pluffgoulu twinning project: *Twin Towns, Twin Histories,* and shuffled through the most recent correspondence.

We can donate to you our exhibit THE HISTORY OF FISH, which you know is very populous in Bretagne, especial in Pluffgoulu. We have the net and seagull, together with some part of boat.

He found Janice in the Conference Room, going through the Protheroe stuff with her placement student. They'd unwrapped a vacuum cleaner, and were examining a cardboard label tied to the hose. Geraint opened a cigar box, full of teaspoons.

"Somebody called for you," Janice told him. "Reporter from the *Post*. Roddy something. Said he'd look in again this afternoon."

He went back to his office and checked his email. There was a message from Mike: *Can I have your policy paper on access and social exclusion. I want to bring it to the Heritage Services meeting on Monday.*

Geraint sighed, thinking of the teenage mothers; on rainy days there might be four or five of them, moping about on the ground floor. They couldn't get the pushchairs up the stairs, so their knowledge of the County's history must end in the late fifth century. Did that constitute exclusion? He got out the draft of his paper and stared at it, wrote: *School Visits* in the margin of the front page, and put it back in the file.

He went to the library and reached down the 1903 volume of the Proceedings of the Archaeological Society. Taking it back to his desk, he felt a flicker of excitement as the book fell open at the familiar, mysterious words:

> *Now Eugenius, together with his sister Brygga, having given up their patrimony and renounced worldly pomp, retired to the remotest part of Armorica, where they built a monastery of stone. About this time Eugenius became blind, and whilst Brygga was tending to him, a white hound came from the wood and stood on the edge of the river, and behind the hound came a stag and a boar. Not long after these events St Brygga resolved to go to Rome.*

He read the passage through again, smiling to himself. That's all there was. All that had remained of St Brygga was a page or so in the Life of St. Eugenius, existing only in a Latin manuscript in the National Archives, and quoted in a paper given to the County Archaeological Society a hundred years ago. That, and St Brygga's Chair above the sea. A life bounded at one end by a slab of stone on a headland overlooking the bay, and at the other by the decision to make a journey. St Eugenius lived out the rest of his life blind and sisterless, surrounded by disciples, working miracles. St Brygga set off for Rome, and disappeared for nearly fifteen hundred years. It was as though she had been travelling all that time, reappearing suddenly.

There was a knock on the door. Geraint shut the book and slid it into the drawer of his desk. Janice appeared in the doorway for a moment, showing the visitor in, giving Geraint a look he couldn't interpret.

"This is Roddy Hughes," she said. "He's from the *Post*."

He looked about eighteen.

"It's a piece on what's available for kiddies locally," he said. "With the summer coming, and the half-term. Things to do on a rainy day like." Geraint got out the leaflets they'd produced for the last Archaeology Day – *Dig This!* – dozens of kids with hammers and goggles smashing boulders of Newport shale into shrapnel. When Roddy sat down, the shoulders of his jacket rose up to the level of his ears. "It's for the Mams really," Roddy said. "What Shall I Do With The Kids Today?" He framed the sentence with quote-mark gestures. He'd been with the paper a year now. His uncle was their main photographer, did all the sports stuff. Roddy was more on the social side, he told Geraint. He didn't much like doing the Magistrate's Court, but you had to work your way up. "What I'm really after is investigative stories," he said, putting his notebook away and standing up, his suit rearranging itself around him. "Disappearances," he shook Geraint's hand, "and even better, reappearances. Know what I mean? Here's my card."

He got through to Lydia just before the Museum closed. When she answered the phone he heard children's voices in the background; she broke off to speak sharply to them: rapid words in Greek.

"I know it's short notice," he said, thinking how little he knew about her.

"It's OK," she said. "I meet you there."

* * *

"Why it's a chair?" she asked him, pushing her glass across the tablecloth towards him. "On a cliff?"

He poured more wine for both of them.

"It's not really a chair," he said. "It's a big limestone rock. It's about the right height to be a chair, and it's sort of curved on top, as though someone had been sitting on it."

"Looking out to sea," she said.

"Exactly. Anyway, it's always been called St Brygga's Chair. Our local Saint. There's almost nothing else known about her. Just that passage in Eugenius's Life. She decides to go to Rome, and that's the last we hear of her." He hesitated, watching her. "Until now," he said.

He could feel the pressure of his secret knowledge, beating like a dull pulse under the sudden anxiety of sharing it. "It's nothing new," he said. "Just that no one seems to have noticed it." The girl brought their food, and he waited while she set out plates and dishes of vegetables. "There's a Life of St Theosebeia," he said. "It was written by Eustace of Nyssa. It's not exactly a best seller, but it's been translated several times, it's a text you can get hold of. No one put the two things together." Geraint cleared his throat, admiring her patience. "Theosebeia was the Abbess of the double monastery at Thessalonika."

Lydia looked at him then, intense and vivid for a moment.

"The Greek connection," she said. "You are interested in these holy women."

"I'm interested in this one," he said. "She fascinates me. Her life is so mysterious; you just see glimpses of it, like looking through smoke, but you know she's someone who's driven by the spirit, by inspiration. Everything about her is out of the ordinary. She represents the magical possibilities of life: the blinding flash that changes everything." He shook his head. "Not easy to explain."

Lydia patted his hand, smiling at him. "Go on with the story."

"Towards the end of the Life," Geraint said, "there's a description of some of the Abbess's companions." He paused. "One of these companions is called Brygga. Well, Briggana, but it's the same name, I'm sure."

A couple sat down at the table next to them, nodding and smiling, Mel Evans and his wife.

"How's Aled?" the man asked. "Saw him play in the Charity Match last month – that knee of his alright?"

Geraint nodded and smiled at them. He looked back at Lydia.

"It says she had come from the far West, and that she *excelled in holiness and philosophy*." It describes how she leaves the monastery, and builds an oratory near Corinth."

Lydia looked up at him. "I was there with my husband," she said. "Go on. There is more?"

"Yes there is. I copied some of it down. Listen." He took a folded sheet of paper from his pocket, smoothed it out on the table:

Sometimes, when thirst seized that noble woman, she would bring modest refreshment to her mouth by the green herbs and moist grass. In that hot country, where the sun is very strong, she discovered a place with a little moisture. She dug it with a sharp stone as much as possible and at night fall she returned and offered God the usual prayers. The next day she came and found the pond filled with water and edible herbs, fed by a never-ceasing spring.

Mel Evans caught his eye. "Very good," he said. "Very fine."

Lydia was watching him with a sort of amused tolerance.

"Forgot the salad," the waitress said, making room for the bowl in the centre of the table. "Sorry about that."

"Edible herbs," Lydia murmured.

Geraint lowered his voice. "This oratory she built," he said. "The Life says it looks out: *across the Gulf at an ancient temple*. He waited for her to say something. "Don't you see?" he said. "There's two things: firstly, it's very exciting to know what happened to St Brygga. She's our local saint, and now we know where her journey ended. But also, the description of her oratory, it's quite precise: the spring, the ancient temple across the gulf." He drank some wine. "I think we could find it, maybe find the very place, or near enough."

Lydia shrugged slightly, the corners of her mouth turning down.

"Maybe," she said. "There are many ancient temples." Her gaze seemed to turn inwards, overcast with memory, like the shadows of clouds on the sea. "Maybe it's possible."

She told him she couldn't stay out late; her mother-in-law was in the house. Geraint nodded, wishing he'd asked her more about herself. On the pavement outside her front door she tilted her cheek towards him to be kissed.

"Do you have children?" he asked, hearing how abrupt the question sounded, shutting his eyes as his lips brushed the line of her cheekbone.

"Of course," she said.

Chapter Two

The Home Farm cattle had been turned out a few days before, and the bright pasture was flattened in aimless tracks, splashed with streaks and loops of dung. From beyond a strand of electric fence a cow watched Geraint, lifting her tail and shooting out a belching jet of black liquid. The crop in the field to his left, a sweep of ten or twelve acres bounded by a broken stone wall at the edge of the headland, had grown long enough to blow in the breeze, swells of light and movement dappling the surface. Ahead of him, the path followed the slope of the ridge, rising to where St Brygga's Chair looked out over the sea.

He turned and waited for Lydia and the children to catch up. The boys had kicked their football under the electric fence, and now were ducking and jibbing nervously by the wire. Lydia found a stick, and hooked the ball back to them. Geraint watched them as they scuffed it up the path ahead of them. He smiled at Lydia, and she slipped her arm through his for a moment, and then withdrew it.

"It's nice here," she said. "It's good for the boys to get out of the house."

The stone was smooth and warm. He sat down and gestured her over, brushing off scraps of lichen.

"Nice chair," she said. "I can see why she liked it, your holy woman."

The boys scuffled past them, punting the football ahead of them. They were very alike, the younger one plump and hardly more than a toddler.

"*Na eiste prosektikos!*" she called out. "*Kleiste ochi epises!*" The boys turned and looked at her. "Bedwyr," she said, "listen to me. Keep away from the cliff." The boy shrugged.

"Bedwyr?" Geraint asked her. "Like in the Mabinogion?"

She pulled a face.

"Exactly," she said. "And the little one is Gwydion."

Lydia turned away and looked out to sea. "He knew all the stories," she said. "My husband, when we first met. It was a sort of courtship, I suppose. I thought that Wales must be full of magic."

"They're very like you," Geraint said.

The ball rolled under the electric wire again. Lydia traced a spiral of lichen with the tip of her finger.

"He died two years ago," she said. "And here I am."

On Geraint's side of the Chair a series of faint parallel grooves had been worn or cut into the edge of the stone. He showed them to Lydia.

"It could be Ogham script," he said, "but it doesn't really make any sense. They're not grouped right." He ran his fingers over a series of marks cut diagonally into the stone. "It's a funny kind of a script. If you wanted to write at any length in Ogham, you'd find yourself miles from where you started in no time. It's as though someone reinvented the wheel, but made it square instead of circular."

High above their heads a skylark released a spiral of silver notes.

"And you?" Lydia said. "What about you? Helen says you have a son."

"Helen?" he asked, noting the faint tug at the thought that she'd been asking about him.

"My mother-in-law," she said. "David's mother. She brought me to the Museum the first time."

Geraint nodded. "Yes I do," he said. "Aled. He's twenty-two. He's thinking about getting married." He wondered why he'd told her that, realising again that he didn't want it to happen, maybe because the boy was just drifting into it.

"And your wife?"

"No wife," he told her. "She lives in London now."

"Did she come here to pray?" Lydia asked him. For a moment Geraint pictured Elaine, spreading a tartan rug over the stone, arranging her handbag, a prayer book, as though setting out a picnic. "Your holy woman," Lydia said. "Did she stretch up her arms and call out to God?"

Geraint thought for a moment. "I think she lived by inspiration," he said. "She suddenly disrupts her life, throws everything up. There's a suggestion that she and Eugenius were well off, from a noble family. They may have been cheated out of their inheritance – there's a wicked uncle in the picture somewhere. But in any case they leave all that, and set off for Brittany." He gestured out to sea, where a tanker was hull-down on the horizon, slipping off the edge of sight.

"Then another revelation – the white hound at the edge of the river – and she goes to Rome. And if she ever gets to Rome, she doesn't stay there either. She goes on to the monastery at Thessaloniki. Think of the distances, the terrible conditions, among strangers. And from there to Corinth. It's as though she's driven, on and on, south and east, driven. Imagine a life lived like that. What was she looking for?"

Lydia was staring out to sea, her lips moving, murmuring something Geraint didn't catch. She turned to him.

"Perhaps she should have stayed at home," she said.

The boys were calling her, and she tilted her head towards them, listening.

"The big house down there," she said to Geraint. "They want to see the big house. It's possible to go in?"

Behind them, inland, the ground fell away into parkland. Ornamental trees gathered in the centre of the shallow bowl of valley, and framed the wide grey façade of the house, whose severe outlines were pulled out of shape by turrets and belfries and dormer windows. Beyond it were ranges of stable yards and barns, a kitchen garden, and the modern car-park. Geraint nodded, getting to his feet.

"If you like," he said, looking at his watch. "It's called Morton House; it's worth seeing." Catching up with the boys, he lobbed the football down the path; the brothers looked at each other, an unreadable exchange flashing between them, and set off after it. "The family still live in part of it," he said to Lydia. "What's left of them. But it's in the care of National Heritage now. We spent weeks here, cataloguing. Nothing very special, family portraits, silver. In a way, that's why it's interesting, just an ordinary nineteenth century estate.

The economic reality isn't masked by culture."

She nodded, although he had the feeling she wasn't really listening, her thoughts still up on the headland or skimming over the sea towards Brittany. The boys glanced into reception rooms hung with dark portraits and balding tapestries. They whispered to each other, furtive and restless. Geraint called them back. "Come and look at this," he said.

He opened a plain small door that led into one of the corridors of the servants' quarters. He and Lydia stooped and followed as the boys rushed ahead, into a domain that extended all over the house, running above or below the formal public spaces, an area that seemed not quite in the same dimension: corridors and tunnels and narrow staircases built into the thickness of the walls, doors that opened into twisting passageways, bare plastered walls and low vaulted ceilings descending into store-rooms. At the end of a low corridor they followed the clatter of the boys' footsteps up a staircase so steep and narrow it was almost a ladder, emerging at the top through a gothic doorway into the expanse of a large drawing room on an upper floor.

Sunlight streamed in through tall windows at the far end of the room. Geraint became aware of two figures standing there, silhouetted against the light. They had been standing talking under the window, and as Geraint and Lydia came into the room, one of them turned to look at them, and then stepped forward, holding out her hand, a girl of eighteen or twenty.

"Hello," she said. "It's Geraint, isn't it?" She smiled at him, her eyes very blue. "You don't remember me, do you," she said. "You don't know who I am."

Geraint squinted at her as she took his hand. She was suntanned and glowing, as if she'd just stepped off a yacht. "I'm Marina," she said. "Marina Ellis." Geraint nodded, remembering. She'd followed him around the house while he'd been doing the inventory and cataloguing, a little girl then. "How's Aled?" she asked. "I haven't seen him for ages. I've just come back from Greece."

Lydia's sons looked over at her then, and Geraint had a vision of heat, and the slim rise of cypresses. She looked as though she had grown up absorbing sunshine, good food, love, money, privilege; as though all this had been massaged into her, so that she was lit by the glow of these things, releasing them slowly around her, like stored heat.

The other figure stepped forward out of the glare of the window, and Geraint recognised Roddy, the boy from the *Post*.

"We meet again," he said. "Our paths cross."

"Roddy's following up a *big* story," Marina said. She laughed, rolling her eyes, gesturing extravagantly.

"Really?" Geraint said. "Bigger than 'What Shall I Do With The Kiddies'?"

Roddy coughed theatrically, glaring at the girl.

"Thanks for your help," he said. "What I told you was in confidence you know." His voice cracked into a squeak. "I'll be in touch." He hurried out of the room. Marina pulled a face.

"Very mysterious. Nice to see you, Geraint." She smiled at Lydia. "Enjoy your visit."

The two boys had been peering into the wide mouth of the fireplace, trying to see up the chimney. They stared at Marina as she left the room, watching her, it seemed to Geraint, with a kind of longing, as though the door she walked through opened into some brighter world.

Roddy was waiting outside when they left the house, hurrying over to intercept Geraint as they crossed the car-park.

"Have a quick word?" he said. "Won't take a minute." He was holding a notebook, a pen tucked into it.

Geraint found his car keys and handed them to Lydia.

"I'll catch you up," he said. He turned to Roddy. "You always work weekends?" he asked.

Roddy shuffled his feet, scuffing the gravel as he waited for the others to move away.

"Not from round here," he said, watching them. "Haven't seen her before."

"No," Geraint said.

"Thing of it is," Roddy said. "Bumping into you here, I thought: we don't want to tread on each other's toes."

"No, we don't," Geraint said.

"More like: share and share alike."

26

Geraint looked at him. "Share what exactly, Roddy? What have you got in mind?"

Roddy cleared his throat.

"There isn't much," he said. "Not yet; it takes a lot of work, you know that. It means a lot to me. Could make my career, you know?" His voice cracked slightly, and he stared up at Geraint, blinking.

Geraint shook his head. He was about to say he had no idea what they were talking about, but something in Roddy's face, anxious, furtive, knowing, stopped him.

"It's alright Roddy," he said. "I don't want to tread on your toes, or pinch your work, or blight your career, or anything like that."

"Good man!" Roddy said, straightening up, beaming at him. "Good man." He started to walk towards his car, turning and calling back to Geraint. "I'll keep you up to date," he said. "It's just I need to be the first one with it. I'll keep you informed, though. Don't you worry about that."

"I won't," Geraint said.

★ ★ ★

That night, he dreamed the suicide dream again, finding himself driving down the same road, the setting somehow alpine, racing along the lip of a valley that dropped away on his left, a corner coming up at the end of a long straight and the same decision: driving at it, hard down. The slight check as the car took the wooden barrier, cracking it open, a thud and tug that he felt at the pit of his stomach, and then he was flying, singing, released, as his past unwound and streamed out like a brightly-coloured scarf behind him. He pressed down on the accelerator and the car yelled with him, the wheels spinning in the air, their voices joining, streaming out behind them in the sparkling air.

Early sunlight stood in a vertical stripe between the half-drawn curtains. Geraint looked up at the unfamiliar ceiling. He moved his hand across the empty half of the bed; the sheet was ridden into ribs and creases, still faintly warm. Getting out of bed, he found his clothes on the back of a chair across the room. There was a desk in the corner, cluttered with books, letters, makeup. A silver framed photograph looked up at him, and Geraint picked it up. Tilting it into the light, he looked at the dark face that stared back at him, a man about his own age, the features heavy; little engrossed eyes. He set it down and crossed to the window, drawing the curtain aside. Below him, pigeons clattered in the leafy street.

He made his way downstairs, passing a painting of a waterfront, a Greek town, fishing boats tied up at the quay. She met him in the doorway of the kitchen, blocking his way for a moment, putting her hands on his chest in a gesture that was intimate and domestic.

"I wanted to bring you coffee," she said.

Behind her, one of the boys called out to her, asking for something. They were sitting at a round pine table, half hidden behind boxes of breakfast cereal.

"Good morning," Geraint said to them, hearing the uneasy brightness in his voice. They didn't answer. Lydia set a place for him at the table and brought him coffee.

"Take," she said. "What you want. You have the possibility of bread also, and jam." She smiled at him and left the room. Geraint looked across the table at Bedwyr and Gwydion. He had forgotten which was which.

"Cheery Pops!" Geraint said, reaching for the cereal. "My favourite."

"It's finished," the older boy said. "There isn't any."

"He ate it all," the little brother told Geraint. "He's greedy, and fat, aren't you."

Geraint sipped at his coffee. Traces of his dream came back to him. He realised that it had left him with none of the usual feelings of dread and oppression. Perhaps it wasn't about death at all, he thought. That rushing flight had felt like soaring, not falling. Perhaps it now meant escape and freedom, not the bitter animosity of the divorce.

"*You're* fat," the older boy was saying. "And stupid. You're fat and stupid, and stupid." The little boy stuck his tongue out. Geraint opened his mouth, trying to think of something conciliatory to say, realising how out of practice he was.

"And you pee in the bed," the bigger boy added, his voice rising to a triumphant shout. "You wet your knickers and you pee in the bed!"

The little boy's face seemed to fold into itself. He ran out of the room, knocking the chair over. They heard him run sobbing to his mother, and Lydia's voice as she comforted him, the warmth of her consolation bringing back the night. Geraint and the older boy looked at each other over the cereal packets.

Chapter Three

Janice was smoking a cigarette in the Natural History store, a room filled with stuffed animals and the stumps of fossilised trees. Bats, foxes, toads and a sheep arranged themselves around her in a glassy-eyed pastoral. She nodded at Geraint, tapping ash into a bird's nest, one of a row of several on a shelf by her elbow: Spotted Flycatcher, Fieldfare, Dunnock. Sunlight slanted in through the high window, forming solid diagonals in the cigarette smoke and the pale blonde of her hair.

"The Friends are coming today," Janice reminded him. "Should be here by now. I put a lot of that Protheroe stuff in the Board Room. The little fiddly stuff. Should keep them busy."

They walked through to the office, passing the Social History store, crammed with baby-carriages, butter-churns and mangles, stooping under three black bicycles suspended from a cross-beam above their heads. The wall to their left was hung with dozens of embroidered samplers. Geraint paused to read one of his favourites: *Life is a town full of streets, and Death is the market where everyone meets* – hundreds of tiny silk stitches to fix that vapid rhyme, and the bizarre inversion of values it expressed, where life is constrained, and Death is teeming, energetic.

"Perhaps they could do one of those naked calendars," Janice said.

Geraint looked at her. "You know," she said. "Fund-raising: like that Women's Institute did. Revealed – The Friends of the County Museum!" She made a sweeping gesture, the tip of her cigarette tracing an arc through the dim air. "Like you've never seen them before!" They pushed open the double doors of the Board Room. "In all their glory!" Janice said. "Good afternoon ladies."

Lydia was at the back of the group, at the far end of the long table, half hidden behind her mother-in-law. She had been holding an enamel chamber-pot, but set it back down on the table, where it rocked back and forth on its base with a faint tinny clicking. She reached out to stop it, looking up and smiling at Geraint.

"What do you think this is?" Janice said. She picked up a wooden case with a series of slots down one side, and a row of knobs or handles on the other. "Beats me," she said. "Can't work it out at all. I'll leave you to it."

Geraint started towards Lydia, but one of the Friends, Mrs Williams stopped him.

"We need your help," she said. "We're stuck. These are the culprits."

She held a cardboard box towards him. She was wearing a bright blue T-shirt with a logo across the front: *Friends!* She noticed Geraint looking at it and turned towards him to display it, pulling the material tight across her chest. "Isn't it good," she said. "My daughter did it for me." She pointed to her stomach: "And here's the Museum website. *The Friends of the Museum!* Isn't it clever." He nodded and smiled, beginning to step past her towards Lydia, but she picked up the box again, rattling it at him. "What style would you call this?" She held out a little white cylinder, two or three inches long. Geraint looked at it.

"We've put them down as cake decorations," Mrs Williams told him, as the object resolved itself into one of the little columns that hold up the tiers of a wedding-cake. "But are they Ionic? You see there's two of these round thingies here, so I don't think they're Doric. We need your expertise."

"Perhaps you could call them Doric-style," Geraint said.

Lydia was still talking to her mother-in-law. He felt suddenly unsure of how to greet her. Their hands touched, and she swayed towards him as though to be kissed, then took a step back.

"I was telling Helen about the big house," she said. "The boys have been talking about it." She grinned at him. "The secret passages, and the little secret doors."

Helen gave a sharp sniff of disapproval.

"Big gloomy place," she said. "What you want to go there for?"
Behind them, Mrs Williams counted out the Doric-style columns." I
see her in town," Helen said, "that Ffion, Mrs Price-Ellis. They sell
the place like that, and keep living there: it's no more than living on
charity isn't it?"

"Estimated date of manufacture," Mrs Williams was saying. "What
shall we say about that?"

"That family of all people," Helen said. "No one asked them
to behave like that. Themselves to blame." Geraint looked at her,
remembering Roddy's furtive tryst with Marina in the big drawing-
room, and the peculiar conversation in the car-park. "My David
worked for the estate for two years," Helen told Lydia. "Your David,"
she added. There was a silence. "I'll organise the tea," Helen said.
"Come and help me, Lydia."

The meeting with Mike went on longer than he'd expected.
When he went back to the Board Room, the Friends were finishing
up, stacking the tea cups, brushing up crumbs of cake and biscuit.
Janice had come back to help, and most of the items donated by the
Protheroe family had been sorted out, wrapped in acid-free tissue and
boxed, ready to go into the store. When he asked Lydia when they
were going to see each other, she frowned, her eyes flicking across
the room towards Helen.

"It's not so easy," she said. "Soon."

★ ★ ★

When he got back from work, the map he'd ordered had arrived,
wedged into the letter-box, along with a couple of bills, and another
letter from the Pluffgoulu twinning committee. He glanced quickly
through the letter – in French this time. Their initial attempts to
communicate in Welsh and Breton had given way to a kind of English
some time ago, and finally now to French and *Sentiments amicales*. He
put the letter to one side, sighing. The twinning arrangement was
about as moribund as it could be, the Pluffgoulu committee replying
to every suggestion with the same indifferent politeness, qualified only
by their deranged recent offer of part of a fishing boat.

He went up to the top of the house. Aled was in his room, lying on his bed, reading the sports pages.

"How's the conversion coming on up here?" Geraint asked him. "The new flat?"

The boy scissored himself off the bed.

"Thought of a completely different approach," he said. "This room's bigger than it needs to be for a bedroom. This can be the sitting-room. Next door, I'll divide it up: small bedroom, en suite bathroom."

Geraint looked round the room, at the cricket bats stacked in the corners, the pile of laundry, the top of the desk invisible under magazines and papers.

"Remind me," he said, "how many weeks until the wedding?"

Aled grinned at him.

"Loads of time," he said, "no worries. *Dim problem.*"

Geraint smiled at him, shaking his head.

"Think of it this way," Aled said. "Soon as we get our own place, you'll be able to let this floor out. Self-contained. You'll make a fortune."

Something seemed to pass across his son's face for a moment, as though casting it into shadow.

"Is everything alright?" Geraint asked him.

"Never better," Aled said, unsmiling. He sighed. "Never better. Just sometimes I feel like I'm in someone else's story. Know what I mean?"

Downstairs, Geraint cleared a space on the kitchen table and switched on the light. He spread the map open and leaned over it, taking in the place-names: *Zevgolatio, Paradisi, Ellinochori, Limni Vouliagmenos* – the syllables smelling of earth and resin. He would ask Lydia to pronounce them for him. The colours of the map rose up at him out of the pool of lamplight: the lucent blue of the Halcyonic Gulf; the sand-shades of the littoral, deepening in tone as the mountains rose behind the sea; winding yellow roads, and everywhere churches, and the little broken pillars marking ancient sites.

He traced a route along the shore with the tip of his finger: here, Theseus killed the robber Sinis, stretching him between two pine trees. Following the coast road, Briggana would have passed ruined shrines to Hermes, and Aphrodite, Isis and Serapis; near Corinth, in a grove of cypresses, the grave of the beautiful courtesan Lais – *more glittering than the clear spring-water.* He pictured the layers and veils Briggana must have pushed through in her mind, through the hallucinatory uproar of the cicadas, watching her feet scuffing the dusty road: the heat, the painted shrines, the perfumed oil. Below the burning surface her consciousness moved like a salmon in the cool swaying of the river, among water-weeds and the pale eidola of hounds and maidens.

"You planning a holiday Dad?" Aled leaned against him, looking at the map over his shoulder. He sighed. "I could do with one myself."

"This is where St Brygga ended up," Geraint said. "I'm pretty sure it is. Somewhere along this bit of coastline here."

Aled leaned closer to the map.

"Corinth," he said. "Budget flight to Athens, then a bus. Couple of hours from the airport, I suppose. Saint Who?"

"I was telling you about her the other day," Geraint said, "our local saint."

"The Lady with the Chair," Aled said, nodding. "Of course you were. How'd she fetch up in Greece then?"

Geraint looked back at the map, thinking of the lines in Theosobeia's Life: "*Looking over the sea at an ancient temple across the Gulf.*"

"Here's the Gulf," he said. "And here's the Temple of Hera on the headland." He traced a line across the blue, imagining the water restive in the breeze, running up the bright shingle. "Liminidhi," he read, his finger touching a place-name on the southern shore. "This is where it must have been. There was a spring here, fresh water and edible herbs. Liminidhi."

"Liminidhi," Aled said, "not absolutely sure I'm with you, Dad."

"Where St Brygga built her oratory," Geraint said. "She left the monastery and came to live here on the coast. She built a stone cell to pray in. She lived on water and herbs, grasses."

Aled pulled a face.

"The mountains behind her," Geraint said. He looked at the coloured contours of the map. "And more mountains across the Gulf, running down to the temple on the headland."

"Doesn't look like much of a place," Aled said. "From what you can see on the map. Pretty undeveloped."

"See these places further up the coast," Geraint said. "They're looking out at a much wider body of water. You wouldn't say: *looking across the Gulf*.... And nearer Corinth you wouldn't be able to see the Temple of Hera. It has to be Liminidhi."

"Probably really unspoilt," Aled said. "I bet they still got fishing boats there."

"I'm not talking about archaeology of course," Geraint said. "A person like Briggana leaves almost nothing behind. That's why it's so fascinating. The traces are so faint, just scratches in the dust."

"But not a bad distance from Athens," Aled said. "We never sold a holiday in this part of Greece. Funny, that. No doubt there's hotels in Corinth, but what you need is apartments on the beach, self-catering, that sort of thing."

"I think they'd had the plague in Corinth," Geraint said. "Not long before. That would have been a reason to come out here on her own."

"I'll look it up at work tomorrow," Aled said. "I'll check the place out. Bound to have a website. Has a nice sound to it, doesn't it – Liminidhi." He nodded to himself. "Has a nice sound."

* * *

Aled rang him at the Museum while he was having a coffee with Janice.

"You free at lunchtime Dad? Come round to the shop. I've been having some thoughts about your saintly friend. St Bugger."

"Brygga," Geraint said. "St Brygga."

Janice sipped her coffee, raising her eyebrows at him over the rim of the cup.

"Only kidding Dad," Aled said. "But seriously, come round. I've had an idea."

Janice slid the magazine she'd been reading across the desk towards him.

"They're looking for a Senior Conservator in Bristol," she said.

"Don't leave me Janice," Geraint said. "Don't go breaking my heart now."

At lunchtime he walked through to the High Street, across the western edge of the town. On his left, the green dome of the hill rose steeply behind the terraced houses. There was a smell of grass-clippings, and the air was full of falling blossom. In the middle of the town, waiting for a gap in the traffic, he looked across at *Holiday Heaven*. The glass front of the shop was plastered with flyers and posters, splashed with stars and exclamation marks, prices scrawled across in black marker: *Manager's Special – Fjords and Fairytales Cruise – £799! Don't Miss Out!*

The door was open onto the street. Inside, the room was chequered with shadows cast by the posters as the sun streamed through the glass. A girl behind one of the three desks that lined one wall, looked round a computer screen at him.

"I'm Aled's Dad," he said.

"Aled's Dad!" the girl said, beaming at him. "We love your son, we do, the best boss in the county; mad he is!"

She got up and called through a door at the back: "Del! It's Aled's Dad come to see him. He's gone to get our sandwiches," she said, turning back to him.

A second girl came in from the back room, smiling at him.

"He won't be long," she said. "Planning a holiday?" She gestured vaguely at a wall of glossy brochures: white sand and fishing boats, girls in bikinis. *The Greece of your Dreams.*

Aled appeared in the doorway, filling it for a moment, hunching over an armful of paper bags. He rustled through the parcels as the two girls bounced and crowded round him, reaching up at him on tip-toes, backing him up against the desks.

"What you got for us Aled? What you got for us?" Aled drew out packs of sandwiches.

"I got prawn salad here," he said. "And chicken tikka. Get off! Get down Delyth – bad girl!" He pulled a face at Geraint, disengaging. "Over here Dad, let me show you this." He swivelled a monitor round, pecking one-fingered at the keyboard. "It's a bit more developed than what I thought," he said. "But there's no British operators going there at all." On the screen, Geraint saw a shingled beach, fringed with stunted palm trees, a line of cafes and shop fronts, striped awnings and umbrellas. "There's a medium size hotel," Aled said. "And quite a bit of self-catering stuff. All Greek, as far as I can see."

He shuffled the mouse, clicking through scenes of fishing boats tied up to a concrete mole, modern flat-roofed buildings, power lines and advertising hoardings. A view of the town looking inland showed the mountains, terraces of vines scratched untidily into the lower slopes, and the granite rise of a massive outcrop, sheer and square, the rock face glowing like steel.

"Acro-Corinth," Geraint said. "Stop there a moment. Look, you can just see battlements along the top there. It was the Acropolis, the citadel."

"Hour and a half from Athens," Aled said.

"Corinth was famous for sex," Geraint said. "In the Temple of Aphrodite, on the top of the Rock, there were a thousand *hetairai* – temple slaves, sacred prostitutes. People came from all over."

"Have to think how to market that," Aled said. He clicked on again. *The Hotel Korinthos,* they read, *with many maisonettes and superiors. New and improved rendering of services for the pleasant detaining of children, for parents is relaxing during the weekends.*

"Bit hard to picture Briggana in all this," Geraint said. "I'd imagined somewhere more remote."

"More remote would be no good," Aled said. "There'd be no infrastructure. You can't start from scratch. You have to exploit what's already there."

"But it's the right place," Geraint said. "She was there, I know she was."

"It's the perfect place," Aled said. "I'm going to talk to Head Office about it. Small-scale, localised promotion, focused; they're going to love it." Gerant looked at him. "Forget package holidays," Aled said. "We've moved on. We make the arrangements, you do the travelling."

"One of yours?" Geraint asked him.

Aled nodded, grinning. "Leave packages to the Post Office – we do holidays," he said, framing the words in quote-marks. "But really, this is so authentic. It's so Greek! We can really push that. Then there's the West Wales connection, your Saint Bugger and all that. We can use anything you dig up on her, Dad. Gives it a local angle. I'll talk to the *Post* – they'll run something for sure. I'm really excited about this." He glanced around the room, lowering his voice. "Never know, could be a chance to get out of all this."

"I have a contact at the *Post,*" Geraint said. "As it happens. I've got his card somewhere."

"Would you like a sandwich?" Delyth called over. "We got too many here."

"And the courtesans," Aled said. "Have to think how to handle that one. How many did you say there were?"

"A thousand," Geraint told him.

"A thousand," Aled repeated. "A thousand slaves of the temple. It's got something, that has. A thousand sacred prostitutes."

Across the room, Delyth stared at them, a prawn sandwich halfway to her mouth.

He walked back to the Museum through a sudden shower of spring rain; big, heavy drops that seemed to have fallen from a blue sky, releasing a smell of iron and rust as they hit the pavement in slaps and splashes, stripping blossom from the trees. The cleaners had been in over lunch-time, and there was a strong smell of wax floor polish in the hall and through the room of early Christian stones. *Preserver of the Faith,* Geraint read, *constant lover of his country, here lies Rufinus, the devoted champion of righteousness.* The Latin script on the standing stone was faint and incomplete; a display board beside it carried an English translation. Rufinus was a contemporary of St Brygga's, he thought, more or less exact. They could have met. He jogged up the broad sweep of the staircase.

It wasn't only plague, he thought, that drove Briggana out of Corinth. He settled himself at his desk, his reflection dim in the blank computer screen. Corinth had been shattered and half depopulated by an earthquake in 521; the plague had followed, along with famine, criminality, and other interventions of the Divine. Of course, it might have been the earthquake that drew Briggana towards the city in the first place, after she'd left the monastery in Thessalonika. She might have felt a sense of the nearness of God in the catastrophe, as though the tumbled ruins were a foot-print, recent, smoking.

Janice came into the room carrying a tray. She handed him his coffee and went over to sit in the armchair. Geraint woke his computer. Clicking open his inbox, he found seventeen new emails waiting for him. He began an email to his opposite number in Pluffgoulu: *Please specify what part of a fishing boat you are offering,* he wrote. *The poop, the prow, the transom, the bilge, the scuppers?*

"How's the book going?" he asked her.

"I've worked out what it is that finally drives him off the rails," Janice said.

He nodded, without looking round. *The rigging, the decking, the funnel, the screw?*

"Off his rocker," Janice said. The point at which he starts to fall apart."

"You got a name for him yet?" Geraint asked her.

"In my head, he's Geraint," she said.

"And he's going round the bend," Geraint said. "Thanks a lot; that's great."

"What happens is, you know there's this woman he's obsessed with?" Janice asked him. Geraint deleted the email and swivelled his chair round to face her.

"The fictional Geraint?"

"Yes. He hasn't said anything to her, but he thinks about her all the time – Madame X. I think I'll call her Luisa."

"Does he have to be called Geraint?"

Janice fanned the steam rising from her coffee. "It helps me picture him," she said. "I'll change it before I send it to the publishers. The point is, he comes across this painting, on a post-card, in a book or something, and it looks exactly like her, only she's naked."

Geraint leaned back in his chair, stretching his legs out. "Go on," he said.

"Well, partly naked. She's got a sort of dress on, but she's topless. She's got the most beautiful tits." Janice evoked them with her hands. "She's wearing masses of jewellery, loops and coils of it – necklaces and bracelets and rings. There's purple flowers in her hair."

"You sure they're purple?" Geraint asked.

Janice looked at him and grinned.

"It's a real painting," she said. "I'm not making it up – *Salomé with the head of John the Baptist*. It's a strange painting. The head is on a big plate, glass or ceramic, and a slave is carrying it on his head, like a porter in a market. Salomé's leaning forward, touching the head with this fastidious gesture, like it was a fish and she was checking if it was fresh. In fact she's pushing up the eyelid, but she's not looking at it. She's in some world of her own."

Janice sighed, putting her cup down. "She's lifting her dress up with her other hand," she said. "Maybe to keep it out of the blood on the floor."

"What blood?" Geraint asked her.

"From the head," Janice told him. "The bugger's just had his head chopped off. There's blood everywhere."

"Right," Geraint said. "What happens next?"

"That's it," Janice said. "That's what happens next. He can't stop thinking about the picture. Now, whenever he meets her he knows that's how she'd look."

"In an equivalent situation," Geraint said.

"Yes." Janice lit another cigarette. "When he sees her, he sees Salomé. He sees this exotic, dreaming creature – naked – in this violent, bloody setting. It starts to drive him crazy."

"And calling him Geraint helps you to imagine all this?"

"Well, it does really. Yes it does." Her student appeared in the doorway.

"I'm off then," the girl said. "Early finish, you know, you said. Keep my strength up." Janice nodded. The girl waited, wanting something. "Am I going to see you later? You coming out?"

"I'll call you," Janice told her. She shook her head at Geraint as the door closed softly. "Only a bit of fun," she said. "Don't start, alright?"

40

Chapter Four

Someone was sitting in St Brygga's Chair. Geraint had jogged up the rise, and he could feel the thudding of his heart as the sea unfolded beyond the lip of the cliff. He stopped to get his breath back. The figure was sitting upright, bundled up in a fleece and a plastic raincoat; he recognised his mother's friend, Rosie. She turned as he approached.

"I always start from here," she said. She smiled at him, a look of mild astonishment in her eyes. "This is where it always begins."

Geraint nodded, pursing his lips, trying to think of something to say. He'd expected to be alone up here. He'd telephoned Lydia earlier; she was busy all weekend – shopping with the boys, Sunday lunch with Helen. He had put the phone down wondering if she was regretting the whole thing. There was a straw basket at Rosie's feet. She had the look of someone on a park bench, about to feed the pigeons. He walked a little closer to the cliff edge. In the bay, the passage of a ship had left a a ribbon of slick translucency across the restless surface.

"It's like a road," Rosie said. "Like a road across the sea. I'd go that way if I could."

"You off on your travels again?" Geraint asked her.

"All set," she said. "I'll call and say goodbye to your mother, and then I'm off."

"I'll drive you round there," Geraint said. "I've got the car at the bottom here."

She was silent as they dropped down towards Morton House, nodding impatiently at his attempts to chat. As they crossed the lawns that ran up to the west front of the house she quickened her pace, trotting ahead of him towards the car park, glancing over her shoulder as she disappeared round the corner of the buildings. As they drove away she leaned back in the seat, releasing her breath in a long sigh.

"Safe now," she said. "I'm making for the borders. Over to Hereford, and then north, straight up the A49." She shut her eyes. "Ludlow, Church Stretton. I might go west towards Newtown, or east towards Telford. Our own debatable lands. Full of windmills, them places are."

Geraint glanced at her. *Windmills*. It would be windmills. She was smiling to herself, murmuring something, her eyes still shut. Perhaps, after all, her strange certainty of purpose made her view of life the right one, in the same way that Quixote's foolish certainty was right. Maybe life is nourished by illusion and deception. In the High Street, he became aware of Roddy, walking fast, intent, pushing through the Saturday shoppers. As they slowed to let a cattle lorry pass, Roddy glanced in their direction and then stared into the car, lit by a startled recognition. In the rear-view mirror, Geraint saw him run a couple of flailing paces after them, and then stop. Sancho Panza, Geraint thought, befuddled by greed and romance. He had a cup of tea at his mother's, but she seemed hardly aware of him, busy with Rosie.

★ ★ ★

Janice called in sick on Monday. Her student, Lauren, moped in the Natural History store, damp-dusting the menagerie. Geraint sent her home early. Elaine called him; they hadn't spoken for a couple of weeks. The bloody car was going to cost two hundred quid to fix; some bloody brisket, she said, or gasket, or something. She was on her mobile, walking; the weather was shitty and there was no sign of the bus. He pictured her, striding, the phone clapped to her ear. He could hear traffic in the background, and the faint crepitation of the rain.

"Where are you?" he asked.

"Chelsea," she said. "King's Road. I'm late. Where's the bloody bus?" She said something he didn't catch; he heard voices, and laughter. "I'm going to get a cab," she said, a male voice murmuring something in response. "What time are they getting here?" Elaine asked him.

"Most of them turning up later," the man said. *"I thought they'd spoken to you."* The voice sounded oddly out of perspective, as though he was talking into the phone.

"How's your mother?" Elaine said. Geraint realised she was talking to him.

"She's fine," he said.

"There's one," she said. "Goodbye Geraint."

Janice was back the next day. He heard her singing in the little kitchen as she washed up their coffee cups: *Who's that girl, running around with you?*

"I had such a good weekend," she told him. "I've really got the plot worked out now."

"Your student was very miserable yesterday," Geraint said. "Everything alright there?"

Janice shook her head. "Silly girl, that Lauren," she said. "Listen to me Geraint. This is really good. You remember about Geraint and the painting?"

"He's still Geraint then?"

"For the moment. Shut up and listen." She lit a cigarette. "You remember, I told you, the picture of Salomé becomes absolutely mixed up in his mind with Luisa, you know, his special friend. He finds out more and more about it; it's a way of getting closer to her. He finds the picture on the web. The original's in Munich. He decides to go and see it."

"Quite a roundabout way of getting closer to someone," Geraint said.

"Well, he's very shy," she said. "That's not the point. He's had a terrible set-back." She looked at him. "They've been getting on OK in a superficial, work-ish sort of way. One Friday evening he asks her out for a drink. She says no. He was half expecting that, but it's the way she says it, the way she looks at him for a moment. It's like a knife under his ribs. He knows that he's starting to die, right there and then, he's begun to bleed to death. He has to get away, be by himself."

"What's it like writing as a man?" Geraint asked her. "How do you find that?"

"What's it like living as a man?" Janice said. "You're a crappy listener, Geraint. Let me get on." She looked at him. "Anyway, it's good," she said. "It gives some distance. You know, Brechtian; to answer your question." She walked over to the window. "He starts

43

to plan his journey. He's never travelled much before. It's spring or early summer, like this, everything clear and light. I think he'll go by train, because it feels safe, but also romantic." Through the open window they heard the faint repetitive drumming of the Cardiff train, carrying to them from down the line. Janice smiled at him, as though vindicated. "Like that," she said. "I can see him. He's leaning his head against the glass, letting the landscape rush through his head. He's amazed by the speed, the luxury. He's always thought of trains as crowded, dirty, strictly for commuters. Suddenly he's crossing Europe, sipping a glass of wine."

Geraint's phone rang: the guy from the University about the inscription on the Rufinus stone. They fixed a date, Geraint making a note in his diary.

"Go on," he said to Janice.

"When he gets to Munich, he's overwhelmed – the spires, the towers, all that baroque." Janice conjured swirling architectural forms out of cigarette smoke.

"There's a huge fountain in the centre of the square, all nymphs and, you know, what are those things? Satyrs, dryads, whatever; rainbows in the spray. Thousands of pigeons beating around him like waves of applause, as he crosses the *Marienplatz*. He checks into his hotel, and then wanders out into the town. It's evening; the light is golden. He feels as though he's walking on glass." She stared out of the window.

"Don't stop," Geraint said. "He should sit at a café on the pavement, watching the world go by."

"He does," Janice said. "He orders a drink he's never tried before. It's green; he doesn't like it very much, but it doesn't matter." They smiled at each other, seeing him. "The next day, he goes to the gallery. When he sees the picture, of course it's huge, he's overwhelmed, it's like she's stepping down out of the painting at him." Janice sighed. "There's a purple flower hanging against her cheek as she leans forward. Her breasts are so heavy and full, there's all this jewellery glinting between them."

"Nineteenth century, this painting?" Geraint asked her.

Janice nodded. "They liked their biblical nudes back then," she

44

said. "He goes to the Gallery several times, like he can't keep away. The second afternoon, he notices there's a couple of men in the room, sinister types. He has the feeling he's seen them before. He thinks perhaps they were there the day before. They're not looking at the painting, they're looking at him. When he leaves, they leave too."

There was a knock on the door. Mrs Williams smiled in at Geraint, gesturing to someone in the corridor behind her. "This way, darling," she said. "Someone to see you, Geraint."

The girl from Morton House, Marina Ellis, came into the room, her glance flicking from Geraint to Janice.

"Sorry about this," she said, "I should have phoned."

"No problem," Geraint said. "This is Janice."

The girl held out her hand, her fingers slim and straight.

"Marina Ellis," she said.

"Marina?" Janice asked.

The girl nodded. "You know, as in yachts?"

"*What seas,*" Janice said, "*what grey rocks and what islands....*"

"I suppose so," Marina said.

"*What water lapping the bow... and scent of pine and the woodthrush singing through the fog,*" Marina looked at her, uneasy, waiting for the punch-line. "*What images return,*" Janice said.

The girl looked at Geraint. "Actually I'm a bit creeped out," she said. "I thought you might be able to help."

Janice stood up, stubbing out her cigarette.

"Catch you later," she said.

"It's that Roddy," Marina said. "Whatsisname, Roddy Hughes." She walked to the window, looking down into the car-park.

"Have a seat," Geraint told her. "Want a cup of coffee?"

The girl shook her head. "This sounds silly," she said. She had that same look, Geraint thought: sunlight, and the bright sea. "You remember he was at my house? The day you were there? He keeps phoning me. He wants to talk to me, arrange another meeting." Geraint nodded. "Not like that. Or so he says," She cleared her throat. "He said there was something I needed to know, something really important, about my family, about the past."

Geraint shrugged. "He's a funny bloke," he said.

45

"I wouldn't have thought too much about it," Marina said. "Like he was trying to hit on me or something, like you said. But it's not really that." She was wearing a bracelet, Geraint noticed, which she was turning and turning, rotating the heavy silver over the bones of her wrist. "I said something to my mother, you know, joking: what's this family secret?" Marina looked up at him. "And she freaked. You know? She really freaked." Geraint nodded, waiting for her to go on. "She gave me this whole lecture," Marina said. "She said people would always try to get at us, spread rumours, try and harm us." She pulled a face. "It's difficult to explain. She was so worked up. It made me think there must be something terrible."

"But Roddy didn't say what it was?"

Marina shrugged. "I didn't want to know. I was trying to get rid of him. He creeps me out, to be honest. It was only afterwards, when my mother went off like that. So then I thought about you, like maybe you'd know something."

Geraint shook his head. He could hear Janice singing again: *Love is a stranger in an open car.*

"Every old house has its secrets," he said, hearing the triteness in the words. The girl nodded, withdrawing into herself. "I suppose I could talk to Roddy," Geraint said, breaking the silence. "Try to find out what he's on about. Would you like me to do that?"

"Would you?" Marina said. "Would you really?"

* * *

The White Hound was just out of town, the other side of the railway bridge, where the road branched right to go over the mountain or straight on along the valley. A hitchhiker stood forlornly at the corner of the driveway, a backpack at his feet, his arm held out. The place was large, a nineteenth century villa, rescued from dilapidation ten or twelve years ago, and now becoming shabby again. Close to, it had a familiar look, though he'd never stopped here. He wondered why Roddy had suggested it.

He was the only customer. The barman pulled a pint for him and then disappeared out the back. The panelled room was long, the windows shaded by trees. There was something seedy about the place,

46

he thought, that probably appealed to Roddy. After half an hour he called the reporter's mobile, but it was switched off.

Glancing back at the building's façade as he left, Geraint recognised what it was that the place had reminded him of. A memory of a holiday in Normandy came back to him, Aled would have been ten or eleven. They'd turned in at a place just like this, looking for lunch. It was back off the road a little, surrounded by the same drooping trees, the faint atmosphere of decay. There was something much deeper than similarity, Geraint thought, between the two places. It was as though there were complex regularities in the world; so you would always find a certain type of roadhouse-restaurant, set among pine trees, on the edge of a certain type of town. The hitchhiker had gone.

When he got home he found Aled and Angela in the kitchen. He had the impression they'd been having a row, but his son got up from the table, beaming.

"They went for it Dad. I told you they would!" Geraint looked at him. "They're sending me to Liminidhi," Aled said. "I'll have to take it as holiday, but they're paying the air fares. Isn't that great? I'm going to take the full two weeks."

"And isn't it great timing?" Angela said, smiling her beautiful smile, just a faint tic of anger at the corner of her mouth. "Ten weeks before he's getting married. And the top floor not even half done."

"You going too?" Geraint asked her.

"What do you think?" she said.

Aled raised his arms in a sweeping, enthusiastic gesture. "It's work though, babe. I will be working, you know. Couldn't have you distracting me, could I?" He turned to Geraint. "I'm going to check out accommodation, what's available for self-catering, restaurants, all that. The other thing I thought: what about twinning with Liminidhi? We've got St Bugger between us, there's a link right there. You're always saying how useless that Pluffgoulu lot are. What you think?"

"Could be," Geraint said, smiling at him. "When are you leaving?"

"Flying to Athens on Monday." His eyes were shining. "Four days time I'll be on the beach. I'm out of here!"

"Wish I was coming too," Geraint said. "At Corinth, in the Old

City, you can see the exact place where St Paul preached to the Corinthians."

"How exciting," Angela said. "Do you think it'll still be there when I finally get a chance to visit?"

"You ought to like St Paul, Angela," Geraint told her: "*Let them marry. For it is better to marry than to burn.*" Aled crossed to the fridge. "Anyone want a beer?" he said.

"Another thing at Corinth," Geraint went on. "Pausanias says that on the way up to Acrocorinth, there's a shrine – a *Sanctuary of Necessity and Violence* – "*into which it is not customary to enter.*" I'd love to see that. Will you try and find it for me?"

Aled straightened his shoulders, giving a mock salute.

"Of course I will, Dad. You can count on me."

"I'm going to miss you," Geraint told him. "Give us a hug."

Chapter Five

Geraint pushed the wine bottle across the table to Lydia; she filled her glass.

"Have some more meat," he said. "Or vegetables; there's more of everything. I've cooked too much."

She shook her head. She gave him that intense look: the one he associated with saying goodbye.

"He came home after they told him that," she said. "What is the words they use? He took his discharge. They sent him home with all his medicines. A nurse came, couple times a week." She took a sip of wine. "Anyway, the first few days it was sunny, he sat outside, took a little walk in the garden. Then he didn't to get out of bed any more, he just stayed in bed." She drank more wine. "I washed him. Everyday, I took a warm flannel and washed him. He was so thin. He was crying, do you know?" She shut her eyes for a moment. "Why am I telling you this?" she asked, not looking at him. "It's grief," she said, so softly that he had to lean towards her to hear. "Grief is on the other side of the door. You think it can't get in, but it can. There it is, in the room with you. Maybe it was there all the time, you didn't see it." They looked at each other across the table. Lydia shrugged, pulled a face. "And of course Helen was there every day, all the time," she said. "What can I do? She's the mother." She finished the wine in her glass and poured herself another. "So my life here has three chapters. First with David, and the children, of course. Then with David and Helen; that's a short chapter, three months. Now I have just Helen. Now it's just the two of us, nearly two years."

Geraint looked at her. She drew her fork across the remains of the meal, setting it down on the plate with a faint rattle. He thought about saying: *You have me.* He tried the words out silently, watching her across the top of his glass.

"You have the children," he said.

Lydia looked up, catching his eye as though noticing him for the first time.

"I can't stay here," she said.

"Doesn't Helen have the children tonight?" Geraint asked.

"I mean I can't stay *here,*" Lydia said, her voice suddenly sharp with irritation. "I can't stay *here.*" She stood up, pushing the chair back with a short shriek on the kitchen floor. She let her breath out in a sigh, her shoulders drooping. "Also, you're right," she said. "I can't stay here either. I need to call for a cab."

Geraint started to say something but she stopped him, raising her hand in a dispirited gesture. "Suppose I stay here tonight. What happen is I go home in the morning and Helen will look at me; she'll say: *The children were asking where you were.* I can hear her. She'll say: *I told them not to worry. Mother will come home eventually.*" Lydia looked at Geraint. "You can't imagine," she said. "I'm sorry."

At the front door, he kissed her. "Surely she wouldn't say *eventually,*" he said.

Lydia started to laugh. "She would, you don't know her. *Mother will come home eventually.* You can't imagine."

She was still laughing as she got into the taxi.

★ ★ ★

With Aled gone, Geraint found himself leaving for the Museum at least half an hour earlier than he used to. He missed the rambling conversations with his son each morning before they both left for work, but on his own there was no incentive to linger. He got up to date with paperwork for the first time in months.

He went over the final draft of his report again, aware of the Museum coming to life around him on the other side of the office door: Gavin stacking chairs in the Conference Room, the kettle starting to whistle in the back kitchen.

Janice and her student were in the staff room, facing each other across the table. Neither of them looked over as Geraint came into the room.

"Transgressive," Lauren was saying. "What is that? It's your favourite word or something."

"Transgression means breaking the rules," Janice told her. "Transgressive desire is wanting something you shouldn't want. And probably can't have anyway."

"I see," Lauren said. "So, *not* like: being able to have something that you don't really want. Or deciding you don't want it after all." She pushed past Geraint, and turned in the doorway, looking at Janice. "What would you call that?" she said.

Geraint looked at Janice. They listened to the girl's footsteps in the corridor, and the slam of the door at the far end. "What *would* you call that?" he asked.

"Piss off," Janice told him.

Elaine called him again that afternoon.

"They fixed the car," she said. "Still making that noise, though. Listen." He could hear a faint roar, like the sea in a shell, and a rhythmic hiss and slap that might be windscreen wipers. "Can you hear that?" Geraint nodded into the phone. When they had first separated, he'd felt baffled by the speed with which she'd disengaged, as though her emotions had simply opened like the fingers of a hand, letting go. Sometimes it felt as though it had happened overnight; that, waking up, he had found that all the emotional possibilities once available had been withdrawn. For him, the feeling of being connected had persisted for months; the sense that you are, when alone, observed, like someone seen from the street, moving across the lighted window of an upstairs room. "Did you hear that?" she said. Geraint nodded. Elaine had always had that kind of tough-minded intelligence in which everything is cumulative, every event modifies what comes next. You can never win against someone who remembers everything. Perhaps he would talk to Janice about it. "Are you listening at all?" she said.

"Where are your cigarettes?" a man's voice said.

"Who's that with you?" Geraint asked.

"What is the matter with you?" Elaine said. "How's Aled? Tell him to come up, next weekend maybe, or the one after."

"He's in Greece," Geraint told her.

Lauren stayed away the rest of the day, and didn't come in the next morning. Geraint found Janice in the Pottery Store.

"Be a little careful, won't you," he said. "When is her tutor coming in to see you?"

Janice shrugged. "I'll give her a ring at lunchtime," she said. "Sort her out. Bit over-emotional."

"Why are some people so bloody tough?" Geraint asked, thinking about Elaine. They looked at each other. "Some women," Geraint said. Janice lifted the box of shards back on to the shelf with a short groan of effort.

"Nothing to do with women," she said. "It's who has the power. Are you coming out? I want to lock up." They walked back to the Main Block across the lawn, passing from sunlight to deep shade under the beeches. "And I'll tell you where power comes from," Janice said. "From not really giving a damn." She looked at Geraint. "You let Elaine tell you what to do because you're still involved. And she isn't. Simple."

Geraint sighed. Ahead of them, swallows dipped and flashed. Beyond the shrubbery a pheasant chuckled suddenly, somewhere out of sight.

"How's our friend getting on in Munich? With the beautiful Salomé?" Geraint asked. "My name-sake?"

"He's getting nervous," Janice said. "Increasingly nervous."

Roddy had sent him an email.

Sorry unavoidable absence Thursday. Very urgent we meet to discuss. Can u be at the same place 6.45 tonight. R Hughes.

At the White Hound, the reporter was sitting at a table half way down the long room, the head of a fox mounted on the wall behind him grinning over his shoulder. On the ceiling above him, a fan turned slowly in the dim air. He got up as Geraint came over, nudging the table and sending foam drooling down the sides of his glass. Geraint came back with his beer and sat down. Above them, the fan gave out a faint creak at each revolution.

"Noticed who you had in the car the other day," Roddy said.

"What is it exactly that you want from Marina?" Geraint asked him. There was a silence. "I don't think she appreciates your dark hints," Geraint said.

"Do you mind me asking where you were going with her?" Roddy said.

"If you've got something to say to her, I think you should just say it; not frighten the poor girl with a lot of insinuations," Geraint told him. To their left, double doors stood open into the dining room, where a couple sat silently opposite each other, bent over their plates, knives and forks held like knitting needles. Geraint looked at Roddy. "Where I was going with who?" he asked him. "What are you talking about?"

Roddy cleared his throat.

"Saturday before last," he said. "You were driving down the High Street, didn't you see me? You had a lady with you, elderly; a bit, you know, scruffy. Mrs Edwards." He glanced at Geraint, his expression sly, pleased. "That's not her real name, mind."

"Friend of my mother's," Geraint said. "I was giving her a lift. What's it to you?"

"Quite a bit, actually," Roddy said. "Mind telling me where she was going? Where were you giving her a lift to?"

Geraint thought about windmills, and absurd quests, and this ridiculous, crafty, posturing creature across the table from him.

"Let me tell you something Roddy," he said. "Your interviewing technique is crap. It's really crap." They looked at each other. Roddy flushed, dipping his head to sip at his beer. Above their heads, the fan had stopped turning, and was letting out a tense drone, like a trapped insect. "Anyway, you tell me something. What are you up to with Marina Ellis? What are you playing at?"

Roddy shook his head.

"It's not playing, you know what I mean? But I don't think you're ready to pool resources, are you?"

"Never mind pooling resources," Geraint said. "I'm going for a leak."

The light in the toilet wasn't working. Geraint pushed the frosted glass window open, the metal frame shedding fragments of rust and old paint. He washed his hands, then glanced out through the window, which looked onto a shabby yard, lined with crates and steel beer barrels, weeds pushing through cracks in the concrete. The light was golden, and the air was warm, scented, as though the window had opened onto another world. Geraint put his foot on the rim of the toilet, stepped up onto the sill, crouched through the open window, and jumped down into the yard. He walked through an archway that led out to the car park. He shook his head, smiling to himself as he got into his car. He felt an extraordinary sense of elation and release as he drove home. Perhaps St Brygga had felt the same weightlessness and hilarity as she set off for Armorica, leaving behind her nothing but an empty chair: absence made visible. Perhaps this was the epiphany that launched all her journeys, the doorway in the forest opening, the light streaming through, the white hound and the white stag summoning her.

He hadn't expected the house to feel so empty. In the silence that met him at the front door, he could hear the fridge, grinding its teeth in the kitchen.

★ ★ ★

He had an email from Aled the next day.

Hey Dad this place is great some really mad people here! Met a girl who teaches English at a language school speaks some Greek she's been showing me around, like this internet café. Why did nobody tell me about retsina before? No sign of St Bugger so far but I haven't given up. You'd like this place you should come here sometime, Aled

He printed it out; from time to time during the day he was aware of checking that the folded sheet of paper was still in his jacket pocket.

He and Janice went for a pint after work, sitting at a table outside the Bull at the edge of the little square around the War Memorial.

"Not exactly Munich," Janice said. "But it'll do." He showed her Aled's email and she read it through, nodding. "Sunny disposition, that boy. Where does he get that from?" She leaned back in her chair, stretching her legs out. "This girl he's marrying, this Angela? What's she really like? Underneath that beautiful exterior?"

Geraint shrugged.

"She's an only child, she works for that estate agent's, you know, the auctioneers. She's bright, very organised, she's doing well. Parents have that shop in the High Street, *Dress-Up*. Don't know what it is about her really."

"I think that's what you call an infectious lack of enthusiasm," Janice said.

"And they're going to live with you? What's that going to be like?"

"Temporary," Geraint said. "They're looking for somewhere."

Janice leaned across the table towards Geraint, looking into his eyes.

"What's up, Geraint?" she said. "You've got something on your mind. What is it?" A group of girls, students from the college, took the table next to them. Geraint glanced at Janice, watching her scan the faces. "She'll be in tomorrow," she told him." Don't change the subject. What've you been up to?"

Geraint thought about that window opening into sunlight, wondering why it always felt right to talk to Janice. He shook his head. In fact, the window had opened onto nothing, had simply left him back at the empty house. The girls at the table beside them were feeding scraps of sandwiches to the pigeons, the birds clattering at their feet, purring in reedy, melodic contraltos. He started to describe the end of his meeting with Roddy.

Janice beamed at him, her eyes shining. "It's a liminal moment," she said. "You went through a portal. It's what pilgrims do." She reached across the table and took his hand. "You're not the same Geraint any more," she said. "I knew there was something. You've been changed forever. You can never go back through the window."

From somewhere beyond the Town Hall a car alarm went off, setting a series of booming chimes rolling across the square towards them in concentric waves. Geraint got up to fetch more beers.

"So that was the doorway to another world," he said, setting the glasses down. "In a pub outside Llanfrychan."

"In the Gents," Janice said. "Why not? Why were you meeting this Roddy character anyway?"

"Do you remember the girl who came to the Museum? Marina?"

Janice grinned at him.

55

"*As in yachts,*" she said. "Yes I do." Across the square, the greengrocer's was closing up, the boy carrying boxes of tomatoes indoors, the owner winding the canvas awning back into the wall. "You have to follow this up," she told him. "There's something going on here. You have to meet this Roddy again, find out what he's up to. Nasty little type, what did you call him: *crafty? posturing?* Got to look after that poor girl. Maybe I'll come with you next time, make sure you don't jump out of any more windows." She patted his hand. "Also, I can use this. For the book. It's what my Geraint is doing in Munich, really. You're walking down the street, and on your right there's an archway you never noticed before, and without thinking about it, you turn through it, and nothing is ever the same again."

She smiled at him. "Of course, you're my Geraint too."

"Hope so," he said.

He called to see his mother. He hadn't intended to stay long, but she insisted on cooking for him.

"Your friend Rosie," he said. "What's her second name?" She put another chop on his plate.

"Take more potatoes," she said.

"Rosie," Geraint said. His mother looked at him.

"It's a funny thing," she said. "I was thinking about another Rosie, just before you got here. In my junior class, the year I retired. Clever girl; they had to take her out of school. And I realised I couldn't remember whether she was Rosie Jenkins or Rosie Webster." Geraint nodded, waiting for her to go on. "There were two of them, you see," she said.

"Do you remember, I gave her a lift here the other day. She was setting off," he said, "on her travels."

"Not the other day," his mother said, "longer than that."

Geraint tried to remember the name Roddy had used in the White Hound: *Not her real name, mind.*

"Was it Edwards?" he said. "Is she Rosie Edwards? Mrs Edwards?"

His mother looked at him.

"I shouldn't think so," she said. "She never married, after all. She wouldn't be Mrs Edwards. When's Aled coming to see me?" Geraint handed her the email, then took it back and read it to her, translating *mad,* and *internet,* and *St Bugger.* "Who's this girl he's met then?" she asked him.

"So if she never married, what would her family name be?" Geraint said. "Rosie what?"

"That's just it," his mother said. "There were two of them. You're not paying attention, Geraint."

★ ★ ★

He'd agreed to spend Thursday morning helping Janice go through the back-log of unclassified material from recent bequests. He found her in the Conference Room, the long table covered in books, boxes, clothing, parcels.

"Ewe pessaries," Janice said, holding up a cardboard box with the fading profile of a sheep on the lid. "You couldn't make it up."

"Ewe couldn't," Geraint said, and she gave him a sour smile. "Where is this lot from?" he asked.

"Williams Blaenteg," she said. "Beginning of last month. There've been three more lots come in since this one."

"We're losing ground," Geraint said. "The bloody stuff is gaining on us."

He pictured the growing volume of donations – a vast mass of glass, paper, rusty metal and rotting fabric; stained, torn, thumbed and greasy, smothered in cobwebs and moving as slowly as a glacier.

"We're going to be overwhelmed," he said. Janice looked at him. He gestured at the table. "This is just people clearing their attic," he said. "We call it *making a bequest to the County Museum* so we can all feel good about it, but we're just a repository for unwanted stuff. Unwanted crap, actually."

What will happen to history, Geraint thought, if everything is kept? We will be lost in an ocean of artefacts, where the exotic is indistinguishable from the trivial, where everything is just a colourless soup. Must write that down, he thought; it would spice up the policy paper.

"I have a new character," Janice said. She pushed a bundle of clothing to one side and sat on the edge of the table, swinging her

57

legs. "A sinister American."

Geraint leaned against the wall, smiling at her.

"Go on," he said.

"There's a little bar in his hotel in Munich," Janice said. "Just off the lobby, through an arch. Three chrome bar-stools, plastic topped bar, the front of the counter done in that buttoned fake leather, like a sofa." She lit a cigarette, sorting through the debris on the table for an ashtray. She reached for a blackened and dented Coronation tea-caddy and flipped the lid open, tapping ash into it.

"Somebody'll end up thinking this is Grandma's ashes," she said.

"The sinister American?" Geraint said.

"Right," Janice said. "So, Geraint's a man of habit. Most evenings he'll spend an hour or so in the bar, after his evening stroll. He likes it there. Two old ladies run the hotel, sisters. They take it in turns behind the bar. He can never tell which is which, but he can't speak German, and they can't speak English, so it doesn't really matter. Fraulein Trost," she said, "and Frau Henker, the two sisters. Geraint has a phrase book, and a Munich city guide. He's conducting a little survey of local beers; he tries a different one every night. *Eine Hacker-Pschorr, bitte,* he'll say, and Frau Henker, or perhaps it's Fraulein Trost, will say: *Dunkle Weisse, oder Kristall?* Geraint doesn't understand the question, so he nods and smiles, and the old lady nods and smiles, and says something else he doesn't understand, and serves him a beer. While he drinks, he reads the label on the bottle, trying to extend his vocabulary. *Eine Königin unter die Bieren.* Another night it'll be *eine Augustiner Edelstoff,* or a *Lowenbrau* – he's heard of that one, you can get it in Llanfrychan."

"I've got some in the fridge," Geraint said. "I quite like it."

"So does Geraint," Janice said. "How confusing."

They grinned at each other. Geraint looked at his watch.

"I need to check my mail," he said. "College should've come back to me by now. Keep the place, I'll be right back."

The University hadn't replied, but there was an email from Aled.

Dear Dad, apart from retsina which tastes of wood varnish, there's ouzo, which tastes of toothpaste I'll bring you some back. There's some strange

58

people here an American they call The Grey Goose after the vodka
I think, wears a suit all the time definitely not on holiday must be a
spook or pretending to be one. Having a strange time here slightly pissed
at the moment to be honest. I might go and look for your Sanctuary of
violence later if I can persuade J to come. All the B ☻

Geraint sent a follow-up to the University, attaching the revised version of the questionnaire. He started a reply to Aled. He was aware of a small pleasure at the thought that his son was seeing another girl, picturing her as Angela's opposite: slight, animated. *Are there any ruins right on the sea at Liminidhi?* he wrote. *Any kind of a spring, or well, or fountain?* He decided he'd finish it at home; he could get the map out and ask more precise questions.

"Look at these," Janice said, shaking out a pair of crushed velvet trousers. She peered at the label. *"Biba,"* she said. "Tempted to nick these."

"Go on with the story," Geraint said.

"So, he's had his usual two hours with Salomé," Janice said. "His two hours with that beautiful body. Her skin is white and very soft, and you imagine that it's moist, like the inside of a petal."

"And the American," Geraint said, "the sinister American?"

"Coming to that," Janice said. "Geraint leaves the Gallery and walks about the town, not going anywhere in particular, not consulting the guide book. He has supper in a dark little restaurant where he's the only customer: *Bratwurst mit Sauerkraut und Kartofflen.* Very cheap; he's pleased with himself for finding the place. Finally he walks back across *Marienplatz* towards his hotel. He's already decided what he's going to have tonight: *eine Isartaler Salonbier.* He likes the sound of that. Frau Henker, or Fraulein Trost, smiles and bobs at him from behind the bar. He orders his beer, and there's a period of smiling and head-shaking. They don't have it! They don't have *Isartaler Salonbier*!" Janice stroked the Biba trousers against the grain of the velvet, raising shadows. "In the absurd intensity of that disappointment," she said, "Geraint becomes aware there's someone else in the bar, a man, sitting at a little table behind him at the back of the room. This person gets up and comes to the counter. He's tall, untidy, wearing a light-coloured suit so creased it looks as though he's slept in it. He has short hair, that square-headed military hair-cut. He nods at Geraint, and orders a drink, speaking German with a strong American accent. *Danke Frau Henker,* he says. Geraint tries to find some detail that will fix the sister's identity in his mind. The old lady fetches down a bottle of vodka for the American, some expensive, exotic brand."

"Grey Goose," Geraint said.

Janice looked at him.

"That's right," she said. "How did you know that?"

Lydia arrived late, with her mother-in-law. The Friends had started on the bequests, and the room was filled with rustling as objects were shuffled, held up to the light.

Lydia came over to where Geraint was standing under the window at the far end of the room. She took his hand, and he kissed her on the cheek.

"You are very handsome today," she said.

Her mother-in-law came over. She was carrying a leather photograph album, the cover scuffed smooth with use, the binding starting to break open.

"I think these were taken at Morton," she said. Geraint nodded, turning the first page of the album.

"The Price-Ellis house," he said to Lydia. "Where we went with the boys."

A family group looked back at him; three men, one young, two middle-aged, standing behind four women who must have been sitting on some sort of bench. A boy and two little girls sat on the floor at their feet. The clothes were 1950s, the men in tweed jackets and pleated trousers. There was a strong family resemblance in the mild, sheepish faces.

"The boy must be Lewis," Helen said. "That was so sad."

Geraint turned the page. In the centre of the photograph a group of tiny figures in white stood on a lawn in front of a grey Victorian façade.

"It is Morton," he said. "Wonder how it fetched up at Blaenteg."

He took the album out of Helen's hands, aware of a faint resistance. "I'm going to keep this to one side for now," he said. Lydia moved away, glancing back at Geraint. When he left the room with the photograph album, she followed him out.

"I'm going to put this somewhere safe," he said, waiting for her.

"I'll come with you," she said. In his office he reached for her, but she backed away. "I need to be somewhere safe also."

"I can lock the door," he said.

"Don't joke," she said. "It's not a joke." Geraint looked at her. "I try to tell you but you don't want to listen," she said. "How do you think it is for me in that house, always with Helen coming round? The boys are happy, school is good, but how do you think it is for me?" She shook her head.

"I meet you and I think: *OK, maybe.* But what happen is: nothing. Nothing happen. Dinner, and sleep together, and dinner again. What do you want, Geraint?"

Geraint cleared his throat.

"You know what *I* want," Lydia said. "I want a new life. I begin to think, maybe I'm with you. But maybe I'm not."

The student put her head round the door.

"Janice here?" she asked.

"Maybe I should go home," Lydia said. "Maybe I should go back to Greece."

Chapter Six

Janice came in to work the next day wearing the Biba trousers, the exotic material pulsing in shades of deep red and purple as she moved. She was elegant and sinister, Geraint thought, like some assassin from the court of Lorenzo the Magnificent.

"Look at you," he said.

She brought a coffee to his office towards the end of the afternoon. He'd been looking through the album from Morton House. Only about half the pages had been used: pictures of dogs, and ponies, and several of the two little girls from the first page, taken over a decade perhaps, ending up in early teenage. In the last photograph the two of them stood awkwardly side by side, one a head taller than the other, scowling at the camera, or perhaps squinting in the sunlight, their poses stiff and reluctant. He showed the book to Janice.

"Lydia's mother-in-law thought that one of these girls could be Marina's mother," he said. "But she wasn't sure who the other one was."

"Who is the third who always walks beside you?" Janice said. *"Who is that on the other side of you?"* She glanced at her watch. "Can you stay on after five thirty?" she asked.

Geraint looked at her. "I've arranged a sort of fishing expedition," she said. "I've asked that reporter, Roddy Hughes, to come here. I told him it was time we pooled our knowledge."

"What knowledge?" Geraint said. "Pool what knowledge? We don't have any knowledge."

Janice grinned at him, tapping the side of her nose.

"That's just it," she said. "We'll get to find out what he knows. It'll be fun."

"You're a nutter, Janice," Geraint told her. "You sit here in stolen trousers…"

"The Stolen Trousers," Janice said. "Maybe that's my title. What do you think?"

"I think you're a nutter," Geraint said.

"Don't be dull Geraint. This'll be fun."

Geraint's computer chimed as an email came in. He went over to his desk to look at it.

"Aled," he said, smiling, shaking his head. "What's got into him? At college I didn't hear from him for weeks."

Just thought I'd do you an e. mobile seems to have died why I haven't been txting. I'm in the internet café. Been doing a lot of sightseeing with J, this is a strange place. I think I may have found something rather amazingly St Bugger-related you may yet be proud of me! Sanctuary of violence tomorrow promise☺

Mrs Williams showed Roddy Hughes into the room. He had a briefcase with him, which he shifted from hand to hand for a moment, his glance flicking between Janice and Geraint.

"I'm Janice Martin," Janice said. "We spoke on the phone." She held her hand out as Roddy shuffled his grip on the briefcase. "And you know Geraint of course."

"Roddy Hughes," the boy said. "Obviously you know that." He looked at Geraint. "The other night in the White Hound. I waited for half an hour."

Geraint glanced at Janice.

"I was called away," he said. "Urgently. Sorry about that."

The Morton House album was open on Geraint's desk. Roddy took a step towards it. He put his hand on the corner of the desk, leaning down to take a closer look. Quite distinctly, Geraint saw him shudder, as though a surge of heat, or shock, had run up his arm from the surface.

"I knew it," he said. "I knew it."

"Knew what?" Geraint asked.

"That you knew," the boy said.

"Knew what?" Janice asked.

Geraint walked round his desk and sat down in the chair. He reached forward and pulled the album towards him, closing it.

"Where did you get that?" Roddy asked. "Those pictures?"

"Have a seat," Janice said.

She moved one of the plastic chairs in front of Geraint's desk and gestured to Roddy to sit down.

"Did you get that album from Morton House?" Roddy asked. He sat stiffly on the little chair, his briefcase on his knees. He looked as though he'd come for a job interview. Geraint shook his head.

"Part of a bequest to the Museum," he said.

"Lot of interesting items," Janice said. She sat down in the armchair under the window, stretching velvet legs out in front of her.

"What bequest?" Roddy asked. "Can I have a look at the photographs?"

"I don't think we can divulge that at this stage," Janice said. She was sitting almost directly behind him, and he had to twist awkwardly round to look at her.

"The bequest hasn't been properly assessed yet," Geraint said. Roddy levered himself round on the chair to face him. Behind the boy's back, Janice grinned at Geraint.

"We should have given you a swivel chair," she said.

Geraint closed his eyes.

"Not a bequest from Morton," Roddy said. "From somewhere else, somewhere you don't want to say where."

Behind him, Janice raised an eyebrow.

"Does it matter where it came from?" Geraint asked. "It's just some family photographs."

"We both know better than that," Roddy said, his smile thin. Janice caught Geraint's eye.

"Don't forget we're on the second floor Geraint," she said.

Roddy half turned to look at her, then shrugged, understanding that she hadn't intended to include him. He cleared his throat, set the briefcase down, leaned back as much as the chair would allow.

"Can I have a look at the pictures please," he said. Geraint nodded, glancing at Janice, and handed the album to Roddy. "Have you identified everyone?" the boy asked. "That's old Price." He turned several pages, murmuring to himself. He tapped the photo of the boy with the tennis racket.

"That's Lewis. These two girls, they're the same, aren't they, the same girls getting older." He flipped through to the end of the album. "Let me borrow this, please," he said. "Or scan some of them."

"What would you do with them?" Janice asked him.

"I'd show them to Marina, obviously. Get her to show them to her mother. That'd sort it out."

Geraint and Janice looked at each other.

"Sort it out good and proper," Roddy said.

Geraint thought of Marina, picturing her in his office, turning the silver bracelet over and over on her wrist. *He really creeps me out.*

"I don't think so," he said.

"Why would you do that?" Janice asked.

Roddy looked at her.

"She'd have to say who those girls were," he said, his voice rising in excitement or exasperation. "She'd have to say who that other is, or rather where she is now."

"There is always another one walking beside you," Janice said dramatically. *"Gliding wrapped in a brown mantle, hooded."*

"Don't know about a brown mantle," Roddy said.

Closing his eyes, Geraint saw a figure in a grey fleece and a plastic rain jacket, looking out to sea.

Roddy shut the album, running his hands over the worn leather cover. He stood up. Geraint became aware of a stillness in the room, the same stillness that he had felt as he climbed out of the window at the White Hound. Roddy's glance wavered between Janice and Geraint. He stooped to pick up his briefcase. Janice moved closer to the door, smiling to herself. Roddy licked his lips. He'd been holding the album against his chest; now his shoulders drooped as he put it back on Geraint's desk.

"Let me just scan a couple of the photos," he said.

"Why's it so important?" Geraint asked him. "What do you think you've found?"

Roddy straightened his shoulders.

"If you don't know, why would I tell you?" he said. "You won't help me, I won't help you. Makes no difference though. I'll get there in the end." In the doorway, he turned back for a moment. He opened his mouth to say something, then shook his head, blinking. He didn't shut the door behind him.

"Not a great exit," Janice said.

Geraint frowned.

"Are we being a bit nasty?" he said. "I can't decide whether he's creepy or just pathetic."

"A bit of both," Janice said.

Geraint opened the album.

"I don't quite know what to do with this," he said. He turned the pages, taking in the labradors, the Shetland pony, the two girls. The mood of the photographs seemed both banal and melancholy; a family with not much to celebrate, mournfully recording itself, documenting the monotony of life.

"Why don't we show it to Marina?" Janice asked.

"We?" Geraint said.

"I'm on your team now Geraint," Janice said. "You told her you'd try and help her. She might know who some of these people are. Don't have to involve her mother. Give her a ring, we'll go round there when we've closed up here. I'm coming with you."

They had to wait at Pont Sais while the cattle were moved across the road, nearly a hundred of them in a straggling column, heads low, udders swinging. A couple of boys were stopping the traffic, and a wall-eyed collie shuttled back and forth along the line. Geraint switched the engine off.

"Been meaning to ask you," he said. "With your sinister American now. Is he connected to the two men in the Gallery, the ones Geraint thought were following him?"

"Good question," Janice said. "He may be. I think Geraint assumes that he is."

Geraint started up and they moved forward as the last of the cattle bumped through the gateway.

"So, what does he think is going on? Why are they doing it?"

Janice sighed.

"I'm not sure. I think he may be losing it," she said. "He's drifting; he's lapsing into melancholy. He doesn't really think about it at all. It's just a condition, like the weather. He's isolated in this awful passion, it's all he can think about." They turned off the main road, along a lane that ran steeply uphill between high banks. "He knows that his return ticket has expired," Janice said. "He should have left a week ago, but it doesn't seem to concern him. He gets more cash out of the hole in the wall to pay Fraulein Trost and Frau Henker, and to buy his dinner, although he's eating less and less."

"Can he tell the old ladies apart yet?" Geraint asked.

"No," Janice said.

"And his beer survey?"

"Deferred."

On their right, an unmade track opened into the road.

"You ever been up here?" Geraint asked. "St Brygga's Chair?" He looked at his watch. "We're early," he said. "Would you like to see it?"

They turned up the track, the car bucking over pot-holes, the tyres scratching on loose stones. They parked at the edge of the wood. A warm wind was blowing through the plantation, the young trees writhing and shivering.

"Do you bring all your women up here?" Janice asked him.

Geraint glanced at her.

"Are you one of my women?" he asked.

Janice opened the car door.

"Give me strength," she said.

They walked up the track towards the headland. "He still goes to the hotel bar every evening," Janice said. "But now he just says *Ein bier bitte* and when Fraulein Trost offers him a choice, he shrugs and smiles." From the cliffs below the headland, the repetitive complaining of the gulls grew louder as they climbed.

"The American is often in the bar," Janice said. "One evening he calls over to Geraint from his table at the back of the room. *Excuse me sir,* he says. *I'd be honoured if you'd join me.* Geraint goes over to where the American is sitting. The man has a bottle of vodka in front of him, and offers him a drink. Geraint notices that there are two shot glasses ready on the table. The man pours him a drink, and they clink glasses."

Janice stopped to light a cigarette, cupping her hands round the flaring match.

"Go on," Geraint said.

"There's something very odd about this American," Janice said. "He's somehow creepy and fake, at the same time. There's something actor-ish about him, but his eyes are," she made a vague gesture, searching for the word, "it's as though they're hot, as though there was fire behind them. It's very disturbing."

"Have a seat," Geraint said.

The stone was smooth and warm in the evening sunlight.

"So this is where your holy woman planned her trip," Janice said. "I can see why. It makes you want to fly across the sea."

Geraint nodded, thinking of Aled in Liminidhi. In the long grass at their feet, little cornflower-blue butterflies flickered amongst celandines and clover. The sea was glassy, breaking into stippled areas where the waves were chopping nearer the shore. "Portals," Janice said. "Moments of leaving, not arriving. And not coming back."

Marina met them at the front door and led them through the hall to a sitting room with high windows at the far end. Framed by the enormous house, she seemed older, more assured, at ease with the soothing attributes of dynastic wealth.

"Mother's in Cardiff today," she said. "I'll make some tea."

Geraint opened the photo album and made room for it on the table.

"Your friend Roddy was very interested in this," he said.

Marina wrinkled her nose, baring her teeth in amused distaste.

"My friend," she said.

"Have you ever seen it before?" he asked. "I think it must have come from here originally."

The girl shook her head. Janice came round the table and sat on the sofa beside her.

"We thought maybe you'd recognise some of the people," she said.

Marina started to turn the pages. She was wearing loops and chains of jewellery on each wrist, producing silvery notes as she moved her hands.

"These are my family," she said, "some of them anyway." She looked up at Geraint. "Why is he interested? Why does he want to know about them?"

"Tell us who you recognise," he said.

"That's Uncle Lewis," she said. "There's a portrait of him in the hall. He died when he was ten, he was kicked by a horse."

Janice nodded.

"Roddy recognised his picture at the Museum this afternoon," she said.

Marina looked at her, her eyes wide.

"This is horrible," she said, her voice trembling. "It makes me feel horrible."

"I'm sorry," Geraint said. Now she looked about ten years old, he thought, the little girl who'd followed him round during the inventory. He turned the page.

"Do you know who these two girls are? There's several pictures of them."

Marina leaned closer.

"One of them's Mother, I think." She turned the page. "Yes, definitely, here she is again. There's photos of her at about this age upstairs."

"And the other?" Janice asked. Marina shook her head.

"No idea," she said. "I hate this, having him poking about like this." She looked at Geraint. "There must be some way to stop him, isn't there? Can't you do something to stop him?" She turned to Janice. "It's probably against the law isn't it? You know, stalking or something?"

Janice nodded. "I'm sure we'll find a way to stop him," she said. She grinned suddenly, her face lighting up. "I'm absolutely certain, in fact."

As they got into the car, Marina waved to them from the front door. Driving off, Geraint watched the slight figure of the girl in his mirror; she stood framed in the doorway until a curve in the driveway took her out of sight.

"I wonder if there *is* some scandal there," Janice said.

"I think there is," Geraint said. "I don't think we helped her very much, did we?"

Janice shrugged.

"The only thing we could do now is talk to her mother, show her this," she said, stroking the soft leather of the album. "But I don't think we want to do that, do we?"

"No, I don't think we do," Geraint replied. He glanced at the album. "Should we have left it at Morton?" he asked.

"I think you could say it's the Museum's property," she said. "We could hang on to it for now, anyway." Geraint nodded.

"By the way, how are you going to sort Roddy out?" he said.

"I'll think of something," Janice said, "something he won't like." Geraint glanced at her as he drove. "Little creep."

"What is he after, do you think? Blackmail?"

Janice shook her head.

"Could be."

Geraint took the long way back to town, the hedgerows stunted and bent by salty winds off the sea.

"Go on with the story," he said.

"OK. Geraint and the American watch each other across the little round table, at the back of the bar," Janice said. She lit a cigarette. "The American pours two more shots of vodka. The table is so small that they're sitting uncomfortably close to each other. Geraint doesn't want to look at the other man, but something keeps drawing him back to those horrible eyes." The car drummed over a cattle-grid. Janice lowered her window an inch, and the rushing air sucked cigarette smoke through the slot, unwinding it from around her like a scarf.

"Geraint knows he is sitting down with a predator," she said. "He feels like someone in a room behind a thin door, hearing the scratching of claws on the other side."

Geraint glanced at her. She was staring straight ahead as she spoke. When she paused, her lips moved faintly as she conjured the images in front of her.

"I don't quite understand," he said. "Where does this predator come from?"

"Grief," Janice said. "The predator is grief. How can you not know that?" She drew a deep breath. "Grief is what is on the other side of the door. Grief is the fire behind the door: you open the door and it rushes in and engulfs you." She flicked her cigarette out of the window, the slipstream exploding it into a shower of sparks. "He can

70

feel the door's weariness. He knows that the fibres of the wood are longing to sag, and splinter, and give way." In the silence she glanced at him. "That's all for now."

"Listen Janice," Geraint said, "This is my bed-time story, you know. This is you tucking me up in bed and telling me a story. Don't let it go too dark, please. You'll give me nighmares."

"It goes where it has to go," Janice said.

Chapter Seven

Angela had never rung him at the Museum before, and he didn't recognise her voice at first.

"Sorry?" Geraint said.

"I waited until everyone had come through," the voice said. "But he wasn't there."

"I'm sorry?" Geraint said again.

"Aled," the voice said, shrill now. "This is Angela. Aled's coming home this morning. I went to fetch him and he wasn't at the airport."

"Sorry," Geraint said. "I was miles away. I don't understand. Did he miss his flight?"

"Of course he missed his flight," Angela said. "He would have been on it otherwise."

Geraint cleared his throat. "You might have missed him at the airport, Angela. Where are you now?"

"He's not at the airport," Angela said. "I've looked everywhere, obviously." Her voice rose. "He's not answering his phone," she said. "I went to the desk, but they said they couldn't tell me whether he'd been on the flight or not. They said they didn't give out that information."

"Are you sure you had the right flight?" he asked.

"Of course I am," she said. "Due in at 9.40. He said when he booked it that it'd mean an early start, but it was cheaper."

"Well he obviously missed it," Geraint said, "the plonker. I don't think his phone is working anyway. I'll send him an email. When did you last hear from him?"

"Day before yesterday," Angela said.

"What an idiot," Geraint said. "I should think he's pretty

embarrassed. Don't worry about it."

"I'm going back now," Angela said. "He's not here, I might as well go back to work."

Geraint woke his computer and went to his inbox. There was nothing from Aled.

Call yourself a travel agent? he wrote. *Get in touch, let us know what's happening.*

He dialled Aled's mobile number, but it went straight to voice mail. He shook his head, smiling to himself.

For the Monday afternoon meeting, someone had produced little plastic place cards at their usual seats at the conference table, embossed with their job titles. There was a carafe of water and glasses on a tray in the centre of the table, and note pads and pencils had been laid out in front of their places.

"As this seems to have become a regular slot I thought we ought to do it properly," Mike said. He drew several sheets of paper out of his briefcase and slid them across the table. "I'd like to work through this agenda, if everyone is happy with that?" Through the open window the blue of the sky deepened imperceptibly. From time to time, globes of thistledown floated past. "Are we on schedule with the new arrangements for the second floor?"

"Pretty much," Nia said. "The farm-house kitchen is done." She looked across at Geraint, who nodded.

"We'll be finished with the school-room by the end of the month," he said.

On Geraint's left, Janice was doodling intently on her notepad, swelling, menacing patterns, like thunderclouds. She looked up.

"Repair of the artefacts is going well," she said. "No problems to report."

The afternoon grew warmer, murmurous with insects. The faint, rattling pulse of the Cardiff train drifted to them on the breeze. Janice was writing something on her note-pad, idly embellishing the letters with loops and curls. *Torpor,* Geraint read, out of the corner of his eye. *Taught her Torture.*

Angela rang him again as he was finishing up in his office.

"Have you heard from him?" she asked. "I don't understand what's going on."

"Like I said," Geraint told her. "He'll be embarrassed, missing the plane, of all people. He may be having trouble finding another flight, or maybe he hasn't got enough credit on his card. He'll be feeling like an idiot; he'll want to sort it out before he gets in touch."

"I don't have any way of getting in touch with him," Angela said. "I never had an address. Why doesn't he answer his phone?"

"It isn't working, Angela," he said.

"Dad says I should call the police."

"He'll be in touch," Geraint said. "Don't worry so much."

That night he dreamed about St Brygga. He saw a small figure, wrapped in a brown mantle, digging in the ground. He could see into her mind, where chasms opened, full of boiling fire. He heard the noise of crowds, and the crying of hounds and eagles, urgent voices from across the bay, and the hollow booming of the surf at the foot of the cliffs. The landscape shivered in the heat, shrouded in resin-scented smoke, like looking through a bonfire. The saint was standing at the very edge of the shore, where the shingle ran down into the water. She was calling across the bay, her voice high and clear; calling, waiting for an answer, calling.

He woke up hearing her voice, and with the sense that there was someone in the room with him. He sat up, his heart jumping in his chest. Sunlight streamed through a gap in the curtains. The voice began again, from the street below his half-open window:

Guide me O thou Great Redeemer...

Geraint went to the window. Below him a dumpy, foreshortened figure that he thought for a moment was Rosie was looking up at him, as though serenading him. Catching sight of him, the woman stooped to pick up several carrier bags, and set off down the street, her voice carrying back as she moved away.

Strong deliverer, strong deliverer...

In the kitchen he made coffee, and washed up the dishes from the night before. He was intensely aware of the emptiness of the house around him, room opening into room. He had an impulse to go to the door and shout up the stairs. The coffee pot started to sputter on

74

the hot-plate.

During the morning he caught up with correspondence, spent an hour with the carpenter in the school-room exhibit, then went back to his office and got out his notes on St Brygga. He thought about her as he'd seen her in his dream, wrapped in a brown mantle. Janice had said something about that, he remembered, one of her interminable Eliot quotes. He decided that he would definitely work up his theories into a paper. He would submit an abstract to *Archaeology* this week. He smiled to himself; it would be a breakthrough in academic archaeology, entirely speculative, backed up by no fieldwork or material evidence whatsoever.

He cleared a space on his desk, and arranged some of the photocopied material. He started to re-read the Thessalonika stuff.

The holy woman was pleasing in speech, and sent forth a sweet and goodly scent. No person was turned away from converse with her. After living for fifteen years in this manner, the blessed woman was freed from present matters and went on her way toward God.

He saw suddenly that though he had always assumed this passage referred to Briggana's death, the text was ambiguous. It might be describing another departure. He realised it was important to him that she had stopped at Liminidhi. Perhaps the ascetic tradition, he thought, the overwhelming desire *to be freed from the flesh, to live freely the life of spiritual and divine persons* seemed more realisable in a hermit's cell, in an oratory looking across the bay. The journey, the life of the road, was engaged, acted on by time and space, intersected by the lives of others. St Brygga's life had been articulated by departures, by doors that opened into another world, but any departure ought to prefigure a destination, the desire to arrive at some final, state close to non-being. He checked his email several times, but there was nothing from Aled.

At lunch time he made a cup of tea in the back kitchen and took his sandwich into the staff room. Janice was reading a magazine at the corner table. She looked up as he came in.

"I've been thinking about Roddy," she said. Geraint unwrapped his baguette. "What's in that thing?"

He lifted a corner of it cautiously, sniffing.

"Not sure," he said. "I bought it at the garage on the way in. What about Roddy?"

"Thinking about this scandal of his," Janice said. "He's dug something up, or thinks he has. But what sort of thing?" Geraint bit carefully into his baguette. From its other end an elongated globule of mayonnaise extruded itself onto his shirt front. He sighed. "So I started thinking." Geraint found a tissue in his pocket and dabbed at himself. "I thought: what sort of thing would fit with what he said, or didn't say?" She looked at Geraint. "I started collecting words. I thought: *disappearance,* or perhaps *missing person.* And of course I thought of Eliot : *There is always another one walking beside you.*"

"In a brown mantle," Geraint said, remembering his dream.

"Exactly," Janice said. "Well done. And that made me think of this Rosie woman you talked about, you know? You said he was asking about her. Who exactly is she?"

Geraint shrugged.

"Someone my mother knows," he said, "on one level, anyway. Bit crazy; don't know whether you'd call her a bag-lady. A part-time bag-lady perhaps." He picked up his baguette, manoeuvring it cautiously, tilting his head towards it tentatively, as though he were about to kiss it. "On another level, I think she's St Brygga reincarnate." Janice looked at him. "What I mean is, if I want to imagine St Brygga, I think of Rosie."

Janice nodded.

"I know exactly what you mean," she said. "I do the same thing with the characters in my book. You have a template from the real world, which defines the outlines of the fictional person."

"Geraint, for instance," he said.

"Well, yes," Janice said. "But you're doing the same thing. You're writing a novel about St Brygga. She exists because you imagine her."

"Don't tell *Archaeology Today* that," Geraint said. "I'm going to submit a paper to them."

"It's a big responsibility," Janice said. "You have magical power over your creations. You conjure them up, and breathe life into them. Thought is made flesh." They looked at each other. "In your case

Rosie's flesh."

"And in your case mine," Geraint said. "Couldn't you go a bit easier on poor Geraint? All that grief?"

"It's for a purpose," she told him, pursing her lips, mocking him. "But you can use your power too, Geraint. You can have St Brygga raise the dead, or walk on water."

Angela rang him again that afternoon.

"I've been trying to get hold of you," she said. "I went to the shop today, in my lunch-hour, to see if he'd been in touch with them. I sort of thought he'd be there."

"The shop?" Geraint said.

"The shop. The agency. *Holiday Heaven.* I thought: he'll have let work know what's going on. But they hadn't heard from him. Delyth said they thought at first they'd got the dates muddled, but they looked it up in the office diary and no, he should have been back yesterday." She was speaking in shaky, emphatic gasps. Geraint realised she was crying. There was a silence. "Did you hear what I said?" Her voice rose. "Why haven't we heard from him?"

Geraint shook his head, wincing.

"I don't know," he said. "I'll phone the airline. Who did he fly with?"

"What good will that do?" she said. "What good will that do?"

Geraint sent another email: *Aled — we need to hear from you. Get in touch.* He texted the same message to the mobile number. He looked up the airline website and got their Customer Services phone number. *Please listen carefully to the following options,* he was told. Geraint listened, pushing button after button on his phone. *We are experiencing an unusually high volume of calls,* the voice said, turning him over to a loop of Mozart. Geraint waited through several melancholy repetitions of the music. *All our representatives are currently busy,* the voice said. *Please try later.*

He found Janice in the Social History store. He realised he didn't want to mention Aled to her for the moment; it was better to push the thought away.

"Come for a pint," he said. "I want to hear what's been happening to Geraint."

"Ten minutes," Janice said.

They sat at the same table in the square, across from the War Memorial. The evening was cooler, and there were clouds massing in the west, behind the Clock Tower.

"The Grey Goose has been asking Geraint questions," Janice said. "All sorts of questions. Is he married? How long has he been in Munich? What other cities does he plan to visit? Has he ever been in the Middle East? In Syria, for instance?"

"Sorry Janice," Geraint said. "I'm in a bit of a state."

Janice watched him, listening in silence as he explained about Aled.

"He's a big lad, Geraint," she said finally. "What was the name of the girl in the email you showed me?"

"Jessica," Geraint told her.

"Jessica," Janice said. "That's right. So, ask Jessica, that's my advice. Bet she knows exactly where he is, right this minute. Stop worrying."

"I'm trying not to," Geraint said. "I had the same thought. You're probably right." He shook his head. "All the same, it's not like him. He's always been, you know, impulsive, but this is a bit extreme."

"He'll be fine," Janice said. "You'll see. Bet you hear from him tomorrow." They sat in silence for a while. "Stop worrying, Geraint," Janice said. "Get your mind off it. Tell me about St Brygga."

There was a faint rumble of distant thunder.

"I've been thinking about the oratory she built," Geraint said. "Was it made of stone? How would she have done that?"

"Not dressed stone," Janice said. "Rough, rubble. The local stone breaks easily, in nice neat strata. She's a wiry little thing, she can lift quite big pieces."

"You're right," Geraint said. "She's competent. Her cell looks good. The lintel for the door would be a big piece of driftwood from the bay, the trunk of an olive tree. It's bleached white and smooth by the sea." Shutting his eyes, he could see every detail. "It's built almost on the beach itself, where the shingle flattens out into sandy soil and wiry grass. The spot she's chosen is quite isolated, several hundred metres along the shore from where the fishermen haul their boats up.

Sometimes she can hear them singing, and when the wind is right it brings the smell of grilled fish." He leaned back in his chair, nodding. "This is fun," he said.

"Told you," Janice said. "Go on."

"She's got the structure almost completed before anyone notices she's there," he said. "The first visitors she gets are little children."

"Fishermen's children," Janice said.

"And children from the village. It's hidden by the curve of the shore, but it's not far. Sometimes she sees woodsmoke beyond the trees. The children don't dare come very close at first. They stand in a line and stare at her."

"Does she like children?"

"She does. She more or less ignores them to start with. She's busy; finishing the oratory, gathering herbs."

"And praying," Janice said.

"Of course. Sometimes for hours at a time. I think she's silent. She stands quite still, facing the sea, her arms raised, her eyes closed. Then she'll seem to come back from somewhere, lowering her arms. She has a sweet smile. The children feel safe with her."

"They start bringing her little gifts," Janice said. Geraint nodded.

"At first they think she must want food, and they bring her a fish, or a piece of bread, but she shakes her head. So they start to bring her plants, wild flowers, sheaves of dried grass." They sat in silence for a moment.

"Better than reality, isn't it?" Janice said. She gestured vaguely across the square. "The imaginary world is as real as all this. It's there just under the surface, one level down. You don't see what's below, but it's there just the same. Fiction is as complex as all that stuff out there. Reality is only what we say it is."

"Really?" Geraint said. "That would be nice."

"Let me tell you a story," Janice said. "This is a true story, OK?" Her rings were tapping nervily against the sides of her glass. "There's this community of Jews living in the Yemen, they've been there forever, a little tiny splinter of the Diaspora, utterly lost, but irreducible as a diamond. Their culture has evolved in strange and distinctive ways over so many generations, but they've never lost their sense of Jewishness. They have no coherent account of how they got to Yemen, but they have a myth which is central to their collective identity. This prophesy tells them one day their whole community will be transported back to the Land of Israel, flying on the wings of dragons." Janice leaned forward in her chair. "Are you paying attention Geraint?" she asked.

He nodded. "Yemeni Jews," he said.

"Right," Janice said. "So, I can't remember if it was after the Six Day War, or Yom Kippur, but anyway, the Israeli government decided that these people were at risk of destruction, and should be brought back to Israel. So they negotiated and persuaded, and in due course sent a fleet of Boeing 707s to Yemen, collected the entire community, men, women and children, and flew them back to Tel Aviv." She looked at him. "So their prophesy came true in an absolutely literal sense. How many sensible people would have believed that was going to happen if you'd asked them in, say, 1890?"

"Trouble is," Geraint said, "I am worried about Aled." He shook his head as if to clear it. "I just am."

That night he discovered a database of nine thousand English language schools in Greece, listing sixteen in Corinth, and two in Liminidhi. He sent the same email to both of these:

I understand you have an English girl called Jessica working for you as a teacher. I'd be most grateful if you would ask her to contact me at this email address as I'm urgently trying to contact my son Aled, who I believe is a friend of hers.

He leaned back in his chair. Framed in the window, a star hung in the pale sky. The screensaver came on, a bifurcating maze of repeating metal pipes and scaffolds. The void was instantly transformed into a world of valves, and taps, and cages.

His mobile was ringing. Reaching into his pockets, scattering papers on his desk while he tried to remember where he'd left it, he pictured the caller on the other end, in a phone booth on a deserted street, linked to him by memory, the face that you were searching for as it disappears into the crowd. The phone was on charge in his bedroom.

"Hello," he said. "Hello?"

"Are you free? Can you talk? The boys have gone to bed, I wanted to talk to you." Recognising Lydia's voice, Geraint realised that for a moment he had heard it as the operator's, calling from the exchange: *I have a call for you from Corinth.* "Hello," Lydia said, "Geraint? Can you hear me?"

"Hello," he said. "Yes, I can hear you."

"Did you think about what I have said?" Geraint took the phone back to his study and sat down in front of the computer again. The pipes rushed at him, then doubled back, boxing up space. "This is no good for me," Lydia said. "You don't listen to me."

"Yes I do," Geraint said. "Talk to me."

"I talk to you," Lydia said. "And you don't listen. I need to know what happens next. I know you're busy, but I don't think you're making plans. I need to know about the future. You don't think about that. With you it's like I said, it's dinner, and go to bed, and dinner. It's very nice, but where is the future?"

"I was thinking about St David's," Geraint said. "I was thinking we could go there next weekend. Have you ever been there? It's beautiful." In the silence, he could hear the faint susurration of her breath. "Hello?" he said.

"It's what I mean," Lydia said. "Next weekend. For you, that's the future." She sighed. "And yes, I've been there. With David. It's very nice."

"I'm sorry," Geraint said.

He went down to the kitchen and got a beer from the fridge, the sharp snap of the ring-pull recalling the evening Aled had announced he was going to Greece. He must have given his office an address in Liminidhi, Geraint thought. He would drop in at lunch-time tomorrow and ask the girls in the shop. He rang Elaine's number.

"Just a moment," she said. Geraint could hear voices in the background, a faint tinkle and clatter, the scraping of cutlery. "I'll have the duck, with red cabbage." And then: "Yes, hello."

"It's me," Geraint said.

"I know," Elaine said. "What is it?"

"Just a thought," Geraint said. "Aled's not with you, is he? He's not up in London?"

"Why would he be? I thought you said he was in Greece."

"He didn't turn up yesterday. He must have missed his flight." He heard the clink of a glass, and the sound of liquid being poured.

"Thanks," Elaine said. "Cheers." He heard a man's voice in the background, laughter.

"But nobody's heard from him," he said.

"If he missed his flight he'd be in Greece, wouldn't he? Not in London."

Geraint shut his eyes, trying to collect his thoughts.

"It's just the airline won't say if he was on the flight or not," he said.

"Give me a minute," Elaine said. "No thanks." Geraint waited. "Are you there?"

He nodded into the phone. "Yes," he said.

"Let me get the hang of this. You're suggesting he got the flight back, and then disappeared, or what, came up to London?"

"Not really. It was just on the off-chance. I suppose he's still in Greece. I don't know what to think. I don't understand why he hasn't been in touch. I can't think of a reasonable explanation."

There was a silence.

"Alright," Elaine said. "There's nothing we can do tonight." Geraint could hear the change in her voice as her attention engaged. "There'll be an explanation," she said. "Call me tomorrow morning, we'll sort it out."

Chapter Eight

At the police station, a printed sign on the door said: *The bell on your left is out of order, please use the intercom to your right.* Below the painted grille of the intercom, another notice had been pasted to the wall: *The intercom is not working.* Geraint pressed the bell. There was a wired-glass window in the door and he peered through this, seeing his reflection until it misted over with his breath. He stepped back, then took a coin from his pocket and rapped sharply on the glass. On the wall to his right, a number of posters were pinned on a board. *Have you seen this man?* Geraint examined the face that looked back at him, features blurred and dissociated, the eyes blank. Below a drink-driving poster, a notice said: *There may not be any officers in this station at the present time.*

His mobile murmured, trembling, in his pocket.

"Hello?" he said, looking into the dead eyes of the wanted man.

"I phoned the Foreign Office," Elaine said. He could hear the ululations of a police siren behind her voice. "I spoke to someone who deals with this kind of thing." Geraint nodded, thinking: what kind of thing is this? "Are you there?" The police sirens were suddenly louder. "I passed on the details you gave me. The Consulate will get hold of someone in Corinth. They'll check with the local police, hospitals, you know." There was a silence. "Where are you?" Elaine was speaking so quietly he had to cup his hand over his other ear, stooping over the phone. "Where are you at the moment?"

The door of the police station opened, rattling and scraping on loose hinges. The policeman motioned Geraint in through the door, and went back behind the counter, lowering the flap behind him. He nodded, chewing, his cheeks bulging.

"Just finish my sandwich," he said. He spread out sheets of paper and printed forms in front of him. *Liminidhi,* he wrote; *Corinth. Not depressed.* "I'll just check this with my sergeant," he said, going out through a door behind the front desk. Geraint could hear a nasal murmur of voices. He couldn't tell whether the policeman was talking on the phone, or to someone with him in the back room. "We'll fill in a Missing Person form," the man said, coming back with more paperwork. "We'll put your son on the database, on the PNC. We'll contact the airline, see if he was on that flight after all; see if he's in this country." Geraint nodded, feeling a small and cheerless vindication. "And we'll do a cell analysis on his mobile phone," the man was saying. "See if it's switched on or off; when it was last used. Whether it's been used back in this country, that sort of thing." They looked at each other in silence for a moment. "Happens all the time, you know," the policeman said. "What you say, he's not mental health, but maybe things got a bit much for him, just needs a complete break. Trouble with the girlfriend, could it be? You'll see, give it a day or two, you'll get a phone-call."

Geraint nodded.

"We'll take it on from here," the man said. "But you keep on trying to contact him. Take my word, he'll get in touch with someone in a day or two."

★ ★ ★

"Geraint's started using an internet café," Janice told him. "In a side street off Marienplatz. The painting has got him interested in art history. He's looked up other painters who've done Salomé: Gustave Moreau, Lovis Corinth, Dali, Franz Stuck."

"Corinth?" Geraint asked, looking up from his desk. Janice was sitting sideways across the big chair under the window, her legs over one of the arms. She nodded.

"Stuck is interesting," she said. "Quite crude images, but he's got this same sexuality, this erotic power that pours out of the girl, like she's on fire: the ecstatic delight that she takes in herself. It burns its way through Geraint. He's becoming transparent. I see him walk down the street, and you can see through him." She picked up a pen and doodled a moustache on a face in the newspaper. "Your son'll be fine,"

84

she said. "He's in some scrape. He'll sort it out and then he'll be in touch." Geraint nodded. "Where was I reading?" Janice said. "A guy turned up in Ibiza, he'd been missing for a year and a half. Everybody was frantic, girlfriend, you can imagine. They were starting to give up on him. A local journalist found him living in a commune. He said he needed to change his life; he'd kept meaning to get in touch, just hadn't got round to it. For a year and a half."

"Aled's not like that," Geraint said. "I don't think so."

Janice shook her head impatiently.

"Of course not," she said. "It's a different story." She gestured at him with her pen. "Aled isn't passive. He isn't squatting round a campfire with a bunch of hippies." She grinned at him. "He's with that girl, do you want to bet? I could tell she was beautiful just from that email you showed me."

"This is my fault," Geraint said. "It was me going on about Liminidhi that got him out there."

"It's not your fault," Janice said. "It's not your fault, and anyway he's fine. He was feeling trapped, and he's broken free. All that marriage stuff."

Geraint looked at her.

"This is crap," he said. "You barely know him at all."

"I've met Angela," Janice said.

"What does that mean?"

"You know what I mean. She's just too, I don't know, perfect. And too big, anyway. She must be six foot." Geraint shook his head, smiling despite the irritation he felt. "Anyway, novelist's intuition," Janice said, pointing her pen at him. "Listen. He called round the Language School one evening, twilight, the sea getting that milky look, like the surface of a pearl. She'd just finished her last class, she was stacking the text books. He tells her there's a ferry leaving for the islands at midnight. She's wiping the blackboard, her back to him, and he sees her go very still for a moment. Then she turns round and smiles at him."

"This isn't fiction," Geraint said.

"I'm not being flippant," Janice said. "When you don't know what's going on, you tell yourself a story." She looked at him. "You've been doing that all day, haven't you?" He nodded. "But you can choose what kind of story you tell yourself. My story is better than yours, isn't it?" Geraint shrugged, knowing that she didn't mean to sound so hard. He scrolled through his contacts and clicked Aled's number. There was a long silence before the answerphone came on: *Hi this is Aled's phone. Leave me a message.* Janice was looking at him.

"Stories are the only way we have of knowing what's going on out there," she said. "As soon as we try to interpret reality, try to understand it, it's fiction; we're making it up."

Geraint set his phone down on the desk in front of him. The thing emanated a sort of tension, he thought, as though it was looking back at him, waiting.

"Something's going on," he said. "I'm not making that up."

When he got home at the end of the afternoon he spread the Greek map out on the kitchen table. Inland, south west of the Gulf, the winding yellow road led through Dafni and Asprokambos; past Nemea, where Hercules killed the lion, strangling it and wearing the creature's skin as a trophy, to Lake Stymphalos, the colour of the terrain darkening as the road climbed on into the high mountains.

"Where are you?" he whispered.

Dedro, he read. *Diminio, Sofrani, Xanthrochori.*

The phone was ringing.

"It's all so damn slow," Elaine said. "Did you talk to the police?" Geraint nodded. "I tried to ring the Vice Consul in Athens. They told me he wasn't available." She gave a short laugh. "Not available. So I googled private investigators. My god, Geraint, those websites. Missing children. All those faces on the screen. *Leanne, aged nine; Euphemia, aged two."* He heard her draw a deep breath. "Anyway, I rang two or three agencies, in Athens and in Corinth, and of course nobody spoke English, or a few words: *I bin ten year in Noo York.* It's just impossible."

"The police are going to look at his mobile phone records." Geraint said. "See when it was last used."

There was a silence.

"It's impossible on the phone," Elaine said. "I couldn't get anywhere."

"I know someone who speaks Greek," Geraint said.

"I think you should go there," Elaine said. "I think you should go to Greece."

He rang Lydia the next morning. He made coffee while he was waiting for her, and googled the address of the Tourist Police in Corinth and the General Hospital on Athinaion Street. Janice rang; he told her he'd be in after lunch. Lydia's eyes searched his face as he explained what he needed. Geraint shrugged, the intensity of her look making him uneasy.

"He's probably off on some ridiculous adventure," he said. "Have to check things out though, I suppose."

Lydia nodded. Speaking Greek, the phone cupped under her chin as she made a note on a piece of paper, her voice harsher and deeper than when she spoke English, she seemed transformed by a cultural energy that released itself in vivid gestures. Geraint heard *Oriste!* and *parakalo*. *Sighnome*, she said. He heard the word *Vretanos* several times, guessing it meant British. She seemed to be being passed from one extension to another, glancing at him as she waited, tapping long fingers nervily on the handset. *Oriste! Telefteia evthomada. Yassas! Efkaristo! Exdaxi.* In the repeated sounds *Ah-leth, ah-leth* he recognised with a sudden shock his son's name. *Efharisto* she said. *Efharisto para poli!* She put the phone down, shaking her head.

"Hospital have nothing," she told him. "Neither Tourist Police. This is good." She smiled at him, and he was surprised by the rush of happiness and relief he felt.

"Yes it is," he said. "You're right. God knows where he is, but he's not in hospital or jail."

"God knows where he is," Lydia said. "God will look after him."

★ ★ ★

The English girl, Jessica, had replied to his email.

Hi Aled's Dad. Haven't seen Aled for a couple of days. I'll tell him to get in touch as soon as I see him. ☺ Jess

"Have you heard from him?" Janice asked him. "You look as though you've had good news."

Geraint shook his head.

"Not really," he said. He read the email again. "This Jessica seems to think he's still there. And there's no record he's been in an accident or anything. So I suppose that's good news."

"I told you," Janice said. "There's always a good version of the story." She looked at him. "All this time you've been thinking: *what's happened to Aled?* But maybe nothing's happened to him; maybe he's making things happen. Maybe he's rearranging his life." Geraint nodded, remembering what the policeman had said to him: *trouble with the girlfriend....*

"Maybe," he said.

"Definitely," Janice said. "I can feel it. He's OK." She lit a cigarette. "Not like my poor Geraint. He's becoming invisible, even to himself. When he walks down the street he's no more than a flicker on the surface of the world, like a fish rising." She glanced at her watch. "Reality calls. Back to work."

In the Museum car park, the wind was blowing strongly from the south, stirring the rhododendrons. Geraint thought about his empty house, deciding to call in on his mother.

Switching off the engine, he heard the faint cheeping of his phone, then Elaine's brisk voice.

"You've got to go to Greece," she said. "Angela rang me up, said she can't get you to take this seriously. I agree with her, we have to do something."

Geraint started to say *I am taking it seriously* but she raised her voice, overriding him. "I've got the two of you on a flight on Tuesday. I'll follow you as soon as this conference is over, Thursday or Friday. Tell the Museum tomorrow; compassionate leave, whatever."

His mother was in the front room, shuffling through a heap of magazines that she'd spread out on the table. She hadn't heard him come in, and he stood in the doorway for a few moments, watching her with a familiar mixture of tenderness and exasperation.

"I know it's here somewhere," she said, as he came over to the table and kissed her on the cheek. "If I'd found it sooner I could have made it for our dinner. Did I know you were coming round?" Geraint shook his head, smiling.

"I don't like to try it from memory. I can't remember if you're meant to add carrots. Or how much cheese to use." She sighed, gathering the remaining magazines into a stack and carrying them through to the kitchen. Geraint sat down at the table. "Is Aled with you?" she called from the other room.

"No," he said, hesitating, wondering what to tell her. "No, he's still in Greece."

"In Greece?" she called back. "In Greece?"

The sound of running water drumming in the steel sink drowned out her voice.

"I may have to go away for a while," he said.

His mother came to the door, drying her hands.

"I'm making us some dinner," she said. "You're getting too thin, Geraint."

"Will you be alright?" he asked her. The wind rattled the shrubs in the front garden. "Will you be alright if I'm gone for a few days? Maybe a week."

"Of course I will," she said. "Listen to that wind. Beti will look in, and she can shop for me on Saturday." Geraint nodded. "No sign of Rosie, of course. How long has it been? Not a word." She smiled, shaking her head. "Not a word."

"Are you worried about her?" Geraint asked.

"Of course not," she said. "I never worry about Rosie. I always know she's alright, she's one of those people." She went back into the kitchen. Geraint heard, infinitely familiar, the pop of the gas being lit. "Would you reach me the flour down, I don't know why Beti put it so high. I suppose you're going to Greece too, are you?"

That night the wind rose higher, rattling the windows in Geraint's bedroom. He could hear the branches of the cherry tree thrashing wildly against the garden fence. At two o'clock he turned the bedside light on and reached for a book.

On the Sacred Way from Athens to Eleusis of the Mysteries are to be found Altars of Pity, Shame, Rumour and Impulse. In these Sanctuaries the priest performs rites which are not to be spoken of, sacrificing to the wind on one night of every year.

Towards morning he dreamed of the black sail sighted on the horizon, and the old man's despair, seeing him fall from the battlements into the bright sea, like a diving bird. It seemed to him that impulse acts like a stone thrown into water: pulses of rumour, consequence, regret sent racing across the surface in concentric circles. He woke thinking his phone had been ringing, but when he fumbled it off the bedside table and clicked the call list, there were no texts, no voice messages, no missed calls.

Part Two

Liminality

Chapter Nine

Geraint leaned his forehead against the blurred lozenge of the
window. He shifted his legs, trying to get comfortable. Below
him, the Alps stretched bony flanks, ribs, across the floor of
the sky. The lower slopes were choked with cloud; Geraint imagined
steep-sided valleys, watery distances articulated by the clanking of bells
as chocolate-coloured cows mooched through the long grass.

"Edelweiss," he murmured to himself. "Nuns."

Angela glanced at him for a moment, then turned back to the
in-flight magazine. Higher up, narrow trails followed the winding
contours of the mountains. Starting in some clouded valley, Geraint
thought, you could drive up into sunlight, the peaks rising all around
you into the blue of the sky, where an aeroplane, this aeroplane,
burned like a star. The stewards came down the aisle, vapidly aimiable,
collecting plastic cups and paper towels.

Geraint's bag was among the first off the carousel. While they waited
for Angela's, he re-read the email that Jessica had sent him:

*You can get a train from Athens airport direct to Corinth. After that
local train and bus to Liminidhi. I booked two rooms for you in our
building.*

Angela was defending her position at the edge of the moving belt,
bracing herself as other passengers pushed and jostled past her to get at
their bags. Geraint stamped his feet, working the journey's cramp and
stiffness out of his body; hours of motorway, long-stay car-parks, the
crowds at Cardiff Airport; finally the islands, Kefalonia and Zakynthos,
tilting up to meet them in the shining sea. Perhaps vertigo is the
desire not to fall, but to fly, he had thought, as the plane banked and
shuddered.

The two of them passed through immigration in a dispersing surge of passengers, up escalators, through glass corridors suspended above teeming traffic.

"This was all done for the Olympics," Geraint said. "Smart, isn't it." He had been noticing the way people's eyes followed Angela as they passed, wondering whether she was aware of the effect she produced. She pulled a face, groaning with effort as she heaved her suitcase on to the rack. She sat down and blew her nose. The carriage started to fill up. She moved closer to Geraint to let someone sit down beside her. Waves of heat flowed in and out through the open doors.

"Sorry," she said. "I was thinking Aled must've had the same thought, about the Olympics. Sports mad." Geraint nodded. He had turned his phone on at the airport, and as the train pulled out it trilled at him. *Chin up dear Geraint,* Janice had texted him. *You'll find him soon I know. Open season on Roddy starts here today. Good hunting to both of us x.*

"We'll find him, Angela," he said.

"We nearly came to Greece before," Angela said. "Summer holidays after my GCSEs. We had all the brochures. Then Dad had to have the operation, and we never did. Never thought I'd come here like this."

The railway was running along the coastal strip, under the steep side of the mountains, beside the motorway, through a dusty, disordered landscape: power lines, solar panels, flat-roofed housing, construction sites; the westward expansion of Athens, pushing a tide of detritus in front of it.

"*Aspropyrgos,*" Geraint read, as the train pulled out of a station. He looked in his guidebook. "It means the White Tower. Doesn't really live up to its name, does it?"

Angela looked at him blankly.

"The White Tower?" she said. "Like in the *Lord of the Rings?*"

"I think we might be on the Sacred Way," Geraint said. "Heading towards Eleusis."

"We saw all three films as soon as they came out," Angela said. "Always just before Christmas. It was lovely." She sighed.

"This Jessica," Geraint said. "She doesn't sound worried about him.

Maybe she can explain. You never know."

"What would she know?" Angela said.

To their left, the landscape became more heavily industrial. On the bright water, tankers manoeuvered where the terminals ran out into the sea. Across the bay, the mountains of Salamina rose bare and steep.

"Eleusis of the Mysteries," Geraint said. "Death and rebirth." Angela shut her eyes. "It's just that in here I feel he's alright." He patted his chest with the palm of his hand. The gesture felt theatrical, releasing a flood of doubt.

"Feelings aren't much use," Angela said dully, without opening her eyes. "You're just telling yourself stories. You don't know anything."

He wondered whether he should give her a hug, and made an awkward movement towards her, which he converted into trying to get more comfortable, crossing his legs as she stiffened away from him.

"Neither of us know," he said. "It's a mystery; I just want a happy ending."

Angela put her sunglasses on, leaning back in her seat with a long sigh.

"Three years in a row," she said. "They brought them out a week before Christmas. It was like a real Christmas thing. When we went to see the first one, *Fellowship of the Ring*, we hadn't known each other long. So after that it was like an anniversary, like having your anniversary at Christmas."

On the seats facing them, Geraint became aware of a middle-aged couple watching them, staring with a kind of mild fascination. His phone beeped at him, a text from Elaine:

Where are u now? I think you should go strt to Liminidhi don't waste time in Athens. Make sure u talk *some text missing*

The train slowed, the drumming of the wheels changing pitch as they crossed the steel girders of a bridge, and suddenly they were suspended above the deeply improbable slot of the Corinth Canal, vertical saw-cut rock sides hanging above a ditch of water the width of a freighter, seventy five metres below.

"Did you see that?" Geraint said. Angela stirred uneasily in her sleep. The couple opposite nodded and smiled.

"Korinthos," the man said. "Korinthos."

Angela woke up, her features puffy with heat.

"We just crossed the Canal," Geraint said. "Out of Attica and into the Argolid."

The couple started gathering their belongings.

"I think this is the end," the man said slowly, nodding his head. "The end."

Angela stared at him.

On the platform, scanning the faces in the crowd, Geraint realised he was looking for Aled.

"Are you alright?" Angela asked him, putting a hand on his arm. He nodded.

"We have to get a local train into the centre of Corinth," he said. "Then a bus."

The station emptied, the crush of passengers draining away into the heat. The local train stood on the opposite platform, grumbling to itself in deep rhythmic vibrations, plastered with graffiti. Time hung in dull sheets, like curtains. When he clicked on Aled's number there was a long silence, and then a sustained, harsh tone. Ten minutes later they bumped their suitcases down a flight of concrete steps and out through glass doors into the glare of central Corinth. Geraint opened the guidebook, staring at the street plan of the town.

He sighed, trying to collect his thoughts. It was as though crossing the canal had revealed a disjunction between past and present. He glanced at Angela. When she had rung him at the Museum a week ago, time had ruptured, breaking in two. What seemed to have been lost was the freedom memory delivers to move about in time, to relive, to reinhabit past selves. Time, which had been seamless, the medium in which we live as fish live in water, had all at once drained away.

Trailing their cases, they crossed the square in front of the station, under the deep shade of palm trees and out into light. The streets were narrow, bright with advertisements, the ambient roar of traffic pierced by the shrilling of scooters, the sudden shriek of brakes. Beyond these perspectives the mountains hung vertically around the town.

"We've been travelling for nine hours," Geraint said. For a moment he saw the lesion of the Canal behind them, severing their return.

"I'm knackered."

"Shouldn't we go to the police station?" Angela said.

"I want to drop the cases first," Geraint said. "Let's get to Liminidhi, find the apartment. And I want to see Jessica." Angela shrugged. Geraint's phone groaned and vibrated in his pocket.

Did u get my txt? Where are you? I want you to go straight to Liminidhi don't hang abt in athens. Answer me when u get this

On the bus they sat near the front, as close to the driver as they could as the vehicle nudged through the traffic. Geraint leaned forward to ask: *Signome, Liminidhi?* The driver shrugged, shaking his head, a gesture repeated by two old ladies in the seats across from them, smiling, one of them motioning forward, further down the road: *Ine kondá! Tha sas dhíxo!* Suddenly, they were out of the suburbs and gunning along the coast road, a hot wind blowing off the Gulf. A pale spine of mountains dipped across the horizon on the far side of the bay. Geraint smiled at the two ladies across the aisle, and they beamed back at him. *Poli oreia!* they said, waving at the brightness that streamed through the windows. *Poli oreia!* Geraint smiled and nodded, leaning back in his seat as the healing light flowed through him.

"We should have gone to the police station," Angela said.

The road turned inland a little, running through coppices of pine and eucalyptus. The old lady plucked at Geraint's sleeve.

"Liminidhi!" she said. *"Edho, Liminidhi!"* The bus came to a stop, the doors opening with a clap of compressed air. The driver leaned round in his seat.

"Get out," he told them. "You get out now."

They found themselves in the main street of the village, the road roaring with traffic. On a shop window beside them, a child looked out of a poster at them, a girl in a white dress, holding a bunch of flowers, her photograph framed by broad bands of red and white lettering: *MISSING. CAN YOU HELP?*

Geraint read through Jessica's email again.

"We have to get to Kato Liminidhi," he said. He raised his voice to a shout as a truck swept past, the sheet of paper rattling in his hand. "She says to follow signs to the beach."

Off the main road, the narrow streets were white and empty, silent in the heat. They walked without speaking for a while, their suitcase wheels drumming on cobbles. The streets gave way to isolated houses, separated by stretches of lemon and orange grove, vineyards, great banks of rustling bamboo shivering in the warm wind, the pavement turning to sand.

They passed building sites and new apartments. The wind was blowing more strongly, howling through the reinforcing rods of half-finished concrete houses. They walked round the side of a building, and the sea opened in front of them, like an eye. Geraint pointed to a billboard on the side of a small apartment block on their left.

"*Halcyonic Apartments,*" he read. "*To Your Comfort and Delight.* We've made it, Angela."

Their apartments were next door to each other and identical, opening off a balcony on the first floor. The woman who showed them in didn't speak any English.

"Mr Panagiotis?" Geraint asked. "The owner?" The woman shrugged and smiled. "*Kyrie* Panagiotis?" Geraint said.

"*Avrio,*" the woman said.

"I think that means tomorrow," Geraint said. "I'll try and get hold of Jessica."

"I'm going to lie down for a bit," Angela told him. "Let me know what's happening."

Geraint sent a text to Elaine, and to Jessica. He lay down on the bed. He got up and opened the shutters, stepping out on to a small balcony that faced straight out at the dazzling sea. On the other side of the bay, the spine of mountains, grey turning to pink, stepped delicately down across the horizon to an elongated headland. Geraint poured himself a drink from his bottle of duty free and took it back out onto the balcony.

"Looking across the Gulf to an ancient temple on the headland," he murmured. "Here I am."

Who have you been talking to? Elaine texted him again. *Have you seen the police yet? Are they up to speed about what's going on have they started their enquiries. What about this English girl? How is Angela coping?*

He opened his case and hung up his clothes. Through the thin walls he could hear Angela moving about next door. He wondered which apartment Aled had been in; it could have been this one. He looked under the bed, opened the cupboard, pulled open the drawers in the kitchen area, but there were no clues, no scrap of paper with a telephone number, a name. He went back out on to the balcony. Along the shore to his left, a sort of home-made beach umbrella had been thrust into the shingle, a wooden pole supporting a circular thatch of palm-fronds. Too jaunty for St Brygga, he thought; primitive enough but too frivolous, although she might have used palm to thatch the roof of her oratory. His phone was buzzing a text alert.

I'm teaching until half seven. I'll come and find you when I'm through.
If you haven't eaten already we could go for a meal? x Jess

He must have slept for an hour or so, waking to the sound of someone knocking on the door. He heard Angela's door open, two voices. Jessica turned to him as he opened the door.

"Were you asleep?" she said. "Did I wake you up?" Geraint shook his head. The girl gave him a strangely intense look. "You're so like him," she said, her grin sudden in the evening light. "Or he's like you. How weird. Have you eaten?"

Angela nodded.

"I need to get to a chemist," she said. "Forgot to pack my sun-cream. Shows the state I'm in. And what about the police?"

"Too late tonight," Geraint said. "We'll see them first thing in the morning. I'm starving."

Jessica was waiting for them in the lobby, stepping out into the street as soon as they came down the stairs.

"Iannis will be back tomorrow," she said, half over her shoulder, as they followed her. "He'll be able to let you in to Aled's room. He's got some of his stuff, unless the police took it. Do you like fish? This place isn't far."

The wind had eased. Jessica was walking so fast that they had to break into a skipping trot from time to time to keep up with her. On their left, the sea had turned opalescent, the line of stunted palm trees on the other side of the road silhouetted over the water. On the horizon, the lighthouse on the headland across the bay blinked palely.

★ ★ ★

"It's through that door there," Jessica said. "On the left. *Toualétes.*"

Angela nodded, leaving the table. Geraint sipped at his wine, looking at Jessica over the top of the glass.

"What do you think happened?" he asked. "You must have had some thoughts about it."

"Of course," Jessica said. "Of course I have." She was silent for a moment. "If he'd had an accident or something, the police would know, wouldn't they? Anyway, they didn't ask me much: when I last saw him, what he was wearing, you know." She looked up at him, frowning, as though trying to reach a decision. "I think coming here made him very restless," she said. "Something he said to me, he said: I feel I'm just starting to live my own life, not somebody else's. Something like that." They looked at each other across the friendly disorder of the table. "He wanted to see everything. He was so, you know, eager." Geraint nodded.

"Go on," he said.

"I don't know how much actual work he was doing," she said, hesitating. Geraint looked at her. "I mean, he was having such a good time. He just wanted to enjoy himself, take it all in."

"Did you see a lot of him?" Geraint asked her, watching her crumble a piece of bread into fragments. She nodded, sweeping the crumbs into a pile as Angela came back to the table.

"Do we want coffee?" Geraint asked. Angela looked at her watch.

"How long will it take us to get to the police station tomorrow?" she said. "How far away is it?"

Chapter Ten

The police station was set back off the main street, facing out onto a small square shaded by palm and cypress trees. On a plinth in the centre, the statue of an Orthodox bishop raised bronze arms in a gesture of blessing or warning.

"Let me get my breath a minute," Angela said. The building was a concrete rectangle, its outline interrupted by satellite dishes. A flight of steps led up to double glass doors below a drooping Greek flag. "I'm dreading this," Angela said.

Geraint put an arm round her shoulder, drawing her towards him in a brief hug.

"It'll be fine," he said. "It's what we're here for."

The doors slid open for them, letting them into a brightly lit reception area. A counter ran the length of the room and behind it half a dozen policemen were working at desks. There were six or eight people on the public side of the counter, a family down the far end talking to an officer. The room was air-conditioned, but the air felt thick, murmurous with conversation, the click of keyboards, the soft shrilling of telephones. Geraint and Angela stepped up to the counter.

"*Kalimera,*" Geraint said. He cleared his throat. "*Signome?*"

A uniformed officer glanced at him, flapping his hand in a gesture of vague acknowledgment. Geraint unfolded the sheet of paper that Lydia had prepared for him, written in Greek and, for his benefit, in English.

My name is Geraint Powell. I am looking for my son Aled Anthony Powell (birthday Fevruari first 1984). He has stayed at Halcyonic Apartments, Liminidhi, Korinthos. He is lost missing. Can you help me please.

On the wall above him, an icon glittered in a gold frame, the Mother of God gazing down at him, her head tilted to one side in grief or premonition, the lanky baby pressing his lips to her cheek. The policeman came back to the counter.

"*Kalimera sas,*" he said briskly. "*Oriste! Na sas voithíso?*" Geraint handed him the sheet of paper, watching the man's face as he scanned it. He nodded at Geraint, folded the paper and went out through a door behind him, reappearing a minute later at the far end of the room. "*Ela parakaló!*" he called to them. "Come please."

They followed him up a couple of flights of stairs and along a corridor. The man tapped at a door. An officer in a more elaborate uniform was sitting at a desk, half raising himself out of his chair as Geraint and Angela hesitated in the doorway. He gestured at two chairs in front of his desk.

"Please," he said. The three of them sat in silence for a moment, the policeman rearranging the objects on his desk: a mobile phone, a packet of cigarettes. He nodded at them, drummed his fingers, glanced at his watch. Geraint cleared his throat.

"My son," he said. The man shook his head, holding up an index finger. Geraint glanced at Angela. "We've gone into slow-motion," he said. She pursed her lips.

"One moment," the man said.

A young man came into the room; they had heard the slap of his sandals preceding him as he hurried down the corridor.

"Sorry to keep you people," he said, beaming at them, shaking hands. "Let's get down to business. We can talk in my office." He looked as though he'd spent the morning on the beach. "I'm Nick, by the way."

"You speak very good English," Angela said. He winked at her, brushing a lock of hair off his forehead.

"I have family in America," he said. "In New Jersey."

Geraint found himself staring at the words *I love Loobey* printed across the front of his teeshirt. What could that possibly mean?

"OK," the man said. "I had the basic detail already and we made some enquiry. I talk to Mr Panagiotis at the Alkionides apartment."

He broke off as a couple of uniformed policemen looked in the door of his office: big, middle-aged men in dark glasses, hung with guns, riot sticks, handcuffs, badges. The three of them milled around the room for a few moments, bear-hugging, boisterous. He hustled them out of the room, raucous voices echoing down the corridor.

"Those guys," he said. "Crazy guys." He sat down at his desk and opened the file, putting on a professional manner, Geraint thought, as you might put on a jacket. "So the first thing: no accident, nothing from the hospital. This is good."

He looked up at Geraint and Angela, "Right?" They nodded. "Also, so far, no evidence of crime." He held up his hand in a traffic-stopping gesture. "So far. We don't rule nothing out, but so far is so good." He leafed through the file, pursing his lips. "So we agreed?" he said. "Good so far."

Geraint became aware of Angela shifting restlessly in her chair. She cleared her throat.

"Not really," she said, her voice cracking. "He's still missing, isn't he? No one knows where he is, do they? I wouldn't call that so good so far." She fiddled with her engagement ring.

The Greek glanced at Geraint, an almost imperceptible movement of his shoulders offering a moment of dismissive male complicity, then turned back to Angela.

"Let me explain what happen," he said, lowering his voice, his gestures soothing and placatory. "First thing, I been in plain clothes division here five years, and these people, they turn up after. Eighty five, ninety percent."

"These people?" Angela said. The policeman held up his hand.

"We get the report from British police end of last week, so now we are beginning, right? We checked the hospital, I been to see Mr. Panagiotis."

Angela nodded. "So you said."

"Mr Panagiotis say he paid, checked out, everything normal." He shrugged. "So now we talk to more people, check hotels. Next week we got posters put up – *Have you seen this person?* Like this." He opened a drawer of a cabinet, shuffling through files. "Like this."

From the handbill, another girl's face looked out at them, monochrome, trapped in the past, orbiting the terrible moment of

102

disappearance.

"You see?" he said, tracing the English word with his finger on the brightly-coloured borders of the sheet. "*Missing.*"

"Have you found her yet?" Angela asked.

He glanced at the girl's name and details.

"Not yet," he said. His phone rang, and he talked rapidly into it. "OK," he said. "Next we send fax to all police stations with picture, details. It's a procedure." He wrote something on a pad on his desk. "So, people, how about mental problem? Depression? Bi-polar? Schizophrenic? Borderline personality? Any psychological history?"

Geraint shook his head. "Absolutely not."

"Medical problem? Cancer? Alcohol, drugs?"

"No," Angela said.

"Mr Panagiotis tell me he's a very happy boy, very nice, very friendly."

"That's right," Geraint said.

"And the English, Miss Jessica, tell me the same thing. Very friendly, very happy, very nice."

Geraint glanced at Angela.

"Everyone who meets him thinks that," he said.

There was a silence. The policeman opened Aled's file; shut it.

"But maybe not so happy at home?" he said.

"What's that supposed to mean?" Angela said, glaring at him. "What do you mean by that?"

"Maybe he has problems? Too much work, too many pressure? Other problem, money problem? Gambling?"

Geraint hesitated.

"There could be things he doesn't talk about," he said. "He may have felt under pressure. Maybe he's been keeping things to himself."

Angela raised her voice, talking over him.

"We're about to get married," she said. "He's completely happy. I don't know what you're talking about." The two men looked at her. "We don't have any secrets. He tells me everything. If there was something on his mind, I'd know."

"There could have been things going on here," Geraint said. "Here in Greece. We wouldn't know. You wouldn't know."

Angela stared at him.

"What do you mean?" she said. "What are you trying to say?"

"I'm not trying to say," Geraint began. The policeman interrupted him.

"It's OK," he said. "This is my experience with these people, the missing ones. Sometimes it's illness, but you say there's no history. So in these cases, it's pressure; too much problems. People say: *I can't take it no more. I need to get my life back.* Sometimes they walk away. They just walk away."

"I don't understand this," Angela said. "Why do you want me to think he's chosen to disappear, that he's just gone off? Why is that a good thing?" She turned to Geraint. "And you're the same."

The policeman shrugged. "This is my experience," he said. "So far, no evidence of a crime. But of course we keep looking."

"Good," Angela said.

He tapped the cover of the file.

"This doesn't shut," he said. "We don't close the file on him."

Geraint turned to Angela.

"Isn't it better to think that he's chosen to go off, of his own accord, rather than something's happened to him?" he said.

"He wouldn't just go off," Angela said. "Why would he do that?"

The policeman shrugged. "We must discover," he said.

It was late morning when they left the police station, stepping out into light so intense that it seemed like a solid surface. At the far end of the street, where the parallel lines of pavements and parked cars began to converge, a square of sea filled the vanishing point.

"I forgot to ask him about the Grey Goose," Geraint said. "Damn."

Jessica was waiting for them at the apartment building, sitting on the concrete stairway that led up to their balcony.

"Iannis is back," she said. "I'll go and find him for you." They watched her as she trotted lightly up the steps.

Mr Panagiotis was tall, in his forties. He shook hands with Geraint, nodding the suggestion of a bow to Angela as Jessica introduced them.

He motioned them up the stairs.

"Room Six," he said, opening the door and standing aside to let them in.

Aled's room was exactly like the others, cool behind closed shutters. It had been cleaned and tidied. There was no sense of a recent occupant. Geraint took a deep breath.

"Were the police here?" he asked. "Did they search the room?" Mr Panagiotis and Jessica consulted for a moment.

"He says they did," she said. "They talked to him, and to me like I said. There was a Greek family here too, but they've gone. I think they probably asked at the café on the front, couple of shops. They weren't here very long."

"Please," Mr Panagiotis said. He waved his hand around the room. "You see what you want. Take time."

Jessica called to them from the bedroom.

"There's some of Aled's things in here," she said.

Aled's stuff was laid out on the bed: books, some clothes, a pair of trainers. Geraint sat down on the bed. He shuffled through the books: airport novels, Gavin Henson's autobiography.

"He borrowed my *Rough Guide*," Jessica said, "and a couple of books on mythology, architecture. And he had a phrasebook. He was really trying hard with Greek," she said, with a sudden grin, "really keen."

Geraint laid the books down. "No *Rough Guide* here," he said. "He didn't give it back?"

Jessica shook her head. She looked in the cupboard; crossing the room, she crouched down to look under the bed.

"Nothing," she said.

Angela was handling the pile of clothes, shaking out each thing, then refolding it carefully: a hoodie, a pair of cord trousers.

"Never saw him wear any of those," Jessica said. "Too hot."

Angela picked up the trainers.

"He got these in Cardiff," she said. "I was with him. They're new, there's nothing wrong with them."

"Horrible," Jessica said. "This hot, your feet turn into blue cheese in about an hour."

"Aren't you teaching today?" Angela asked her. Jessica shook her head.

"Later this afternoon," she said. "They come to me after school."

Geraint leafed through the books again: *The Goldhagen Imperative; The Trinity Code; The Reykavik Protocol.* Something had been written in pencil on the inside of a front cover. Geraint squinted at it. The lettering was tiny, but it was Aled's handwriting: *Love is making me thin(k).* He passed the book to Angela. After a moment she pressed the open book over her face, drawing in a deep breath. Geraint and Jessica looked at each other over her bowed shoulders.

Angela put the book down on the bed and got up.

"I'll be back in a minute," she said.

"What was it?" Jessica asked him. "What did you see?"

Geraint handed her the book. She bit her lip, her eyes suddenly very bright. Angela reappeared in the doorway.

"Excuse me," she said. "I want that."

She took the book from Jessica, snatching at it as though she expected it to be withheld, and hurried out of the room.

"I don't understand any of this," Geraint said. "None of this makes any sense." He got up and opened the shutters on to the balcony, the same view of the headland, the temple across the bay. "Why is this stuff here? Why did he leave it behind? Where's the rest of his stuff?"

Jessica looked at him.

"Took it with him, I suppose. I didn't see him packing up. We hadn't seen each other for a couple of days before he left."

"But you saw a lot of each other before that," he said quietly. She nodded. "Why didn't you see him the last couple of days? Did you have a row?"

"Not exactly," she said. "No, not a row."

"Start at the beginning," Geraint said. "How did you meet him?"

"At the internet café," she said, "in town. I use it quite a bit. He just came up and started talking to me. You know how he is." Geraint nodded.

"Go on," he said.

"Is he planning to marry that girl?" Jessica said, glancing at the door.

"So it seems," Geraint said. "I don't know. She's certainly planning to marry him." He put his hand on the pile of clothes that Angela had folded, smoothing the soft grey wool of the sweater. "You're right. These are all too warm to wear here." They looked at each other. "What's going on? This isn't a joke. Do you know where he is?"

Jessica shook her head. "I don't know," she said, her voice rising. "I swear I don't know. Please believe me."

Geraint sighed, watching her. "Alright," he said. He picked up the trainers. "If you were coming back to Britain you'd bring these things with you, wouldn't you?" he said slowly. She nodded. "But maybe not if you were planning to stay here in Greece," he said, feeling the pressure of a strange elation rising in him, "not if you were planning to travel light."

"Iannis didn't see him go," Jessica said. "I asked him. He said Aled left very early in the morning, settled up the night before. Nobody actually saw him go."

"Where do you think he is, Jessica?" Geraint asked.

"I think he's somewhere not far," the girl said, speaking so softly that Geraint had to lean towards her to catch what she was saying. "I can feel him."

They looked up as Angela came back into the room, glancing at each other, aware of the pull of a subtle and intimate complicity. Angela began gathering Aled's belongings together. She had re-done her make-up.

"I'm going to take his things to my room," she said.

"Go on," Geraint said when they were alone again. "You were telling me about how you met him."

"We just clicked," Jessica said. "We made such a strong connection. He was so happy about being here. He was such fun to be around, you know how he is."

Geraint nodded, watching her. It was as though Aled was in the room with them, he thought, reflected in her glistening smile, shining out of her eyes. "He wanted to know about everything," she said. "He borrowed books off me, he read up about the sites. We went to

Acrocorinth, and Mycenae, and Ancient Corinth." She gestured at the open windows overlooking the sea, "and the sanctuary of Hera on the headland, over there across the bay."

Geraint stared at her. "He sent me emails," he said. "But he didn't tell me what he was doing. I never knew he was interested. It just doesn't sound like him."

"He talked about you," she said. "He told me about your Welsh saint. He said you were on a quest." She looked at Geraint. "He said he was discovering himself. He said from now on he was going to live his own life, not someone else's."

Mr Panagiotis appeared in the doorway. He said something to Jessica, who nodded.

"*Endaxi,*" she said. "No problem. He wants the room," she said to Geraint. "If we're finished. He has a family arriving this afternoon."

Geraint nodded, getting to his feet. He felt suddenly exhausted. He looked around the room, searching for something else: some message from his son, something they'd missed in these plain white walls and brick floors. They walked out on to the balcony. The wind was blowing again, the sea splashed white with cresting waves. To their right, a freighter was nosing its way towards the invisible notch of the Canal. They stood together for a moment, looking out at the headland across the bay.

"I've imagined this place so often," Geraint said, "I wasn't sure I'd ever actually get here."

"Aled knew you would," Jessica said. "He said you'd follow your holy woman all the way. You know he found out something about her at Ancient Corinth? He never said what. Did he tell you?" Geraint shook his head.

"Only that he'd found something. He didn't send any more emails after that."

The freighter let out a long, melancholy bass note on its fog-horn.

"I'm going up into town to teach at four thirty," Jessica said. "You could come with me if you wanted the internet café." Geraint nodded, looking out to sea. "I'll see you later then," she said.

Geraint walked to the water's edge, the bright shingle rasping under his feet. There was a piece of driftwood at his feet and he picked it up; it was olive wood, smooth and bent like an elbow. Raising it above his head he threw it in a high arc out to sea, watching it fall. He walked along the beach in the direction of Corinth and the Canal. To his right, across the shore road, the view inland was blocked by a ribbon of cafés and bars. Across the bay the mountains, filling half the sky over Corinth, stepped down the horizon to the headland and the sanctuary of Hera.

Just ahead of him, the shingle was scored into a furrow by water trickling out of a concrete pipe. Geraint thought of Briggana's never-ceasing spring, her breakfasts of herbs and grass. Her oratory might have been here, right here, under the bright awning of this shop selling beach-balls and inflatable dolphins. No canal cut through the Isthmus in her day of course, although the Emperor Nero had begun digging four hundred years earlier, ceremonially opening the work with a golden trowel. Boats were dragged four miles overland along the paved way of the *diolkos,* and Briggana might have heard the rumble of wooden rollers, the straining ropes, the displaced ships with painted eyes wide open on their prows. Geraint tried to imagine that strange teeming world of the past that she inhabited, the sunlight shadowed by old gods still climbing down from Olympus, elderly emperors succeeding each other in Byzantium: Zeno, Basiliscus, Anastasius, Justinian. A world of purges, persecutions, miracles, feuds between pagans, Jews, Christians, Monophysites and Orthodox.

He found a café that was still serving lunch, and sat at a table on the pavement, looking out to sea while an old man brought him bread and olives. His phone buzzed while he was finishing his meal, a text from Elaine:

Arriving Athens Thursday 13.00H your time. Will go to Consulate before coming to you. What progress are you making?

He paid and left.

Angela wanted to go back to the police station.

"I want to see that detective, Kazantsakis," she said. "Nick. He said to call him any time."

Geraint shrugged.

"I think he meant if we had something new to tell him," he said.

109

They crossed the children's playground, where a wobbly toddler tottered through the sand to where his mother crouched, arms outstretched for him, cooing: *"Ela! Ela! Agápe mou!"*

"Agápe mou!" Jessica said, smiling back at them. *"My love."* She stopped at the corner, waiting for them to catch up. "This road will take us past the internet café."

"This Grey Goose that Aled talked about in his emails," Geraint said. "What's that all about? Who is he?"

"The Grey what?" Angela said.

"He might be there now," Jessica said. "He's often there."

"Who are you talking about?" Angela said.

"Don't know what to say about him really," Jessica said. "American; seems to have a lot of time on his hands. Can't say I like him very much, a bit creepy. Very keen to please though, always offering to buy us drinks."

"Us?" Angela said. "Who's us?"

"Aled mentioned him a couple of times," Geraint said.

"Not to me," Angela said.

"Aled was a bit intrigued by him," Jessica said. "Thought he might be a spy, you know, CIA."

"That's something we need to tell the police then," Angela said.

Jessica shrugged. "It was sort of a joke," she said. "What would the CIA want in Liminidhi?"

"Isn't that for the police to find out?"

"Let's see if he's there," Geraint said. "We can check him out ourselves."

Jessica opened the door for them, glancing round the room, shaking her head. "He's not here," she said.

One side of the room was taken up by coffee machines and a big cool-cupboard. There were half a dozen terminals round the other walls. A plump boy got up from behind a till at the far end of the room, beaming at Jessica, his arms raised in a gesture of welcome.

"These are my friends," she said, grinning at him, and the boy smiled, shaking hands with Geraint and kissing Angela on the cheek. "This is Aled's father," Jessica said. The teenager beamed delightedly and shook Geraint's hand again. Jessica looked at her watch.

"I have to go," she said. "Shall we have a drink afterwards? I'll be finished by about eight, what do you think?"

"I'm going to the police station," Angela said. "And I want an early night."

"That would be great," Geraint said. "Eight o'clock."

Dear Geraint I've been thinking of you so much, Janice had written. Geraint sat up in the swivel chair, touched by the tenderness of her words. The boy appeared at his shoulder, handing him a little cup of coffee.

"For you," he said. "From me."

I wish I could be there. You have to email me every day and tell me everything that happens. Geraint sipped at the muddy sweet coffee. *I really feel that I'll be able to help, so please email me every day. I wish I could just fly out and be there but I suppose somebody has got to stay on board the Ship of Fools, and I seem to have been appointed skeleton crew. I so want to know what's going on with you and how you're feeling, but I'll just have to wait until I hear from you. In the meantime, I'll update you with some of my own nonsense. Firstly, with your namesake Geraint. OK, so, my sinister American, my Grey Goose, is waiting for him in the little hotel bar the following evening, and this time he insists on taking Geraint out for a meal. "On me," he says. "Or you might say, on the Company." Geraint has a feeling that the Company is a phrase people use when they mean the CIA, but then he thinks perhaps he's being melodramatic, that the man's emphasis was ironic. They're walking quite fast, and they're soon in a part of the city Geraint doesn't recognise, the streets narrow, the houses half-timbered and leaning towards each other so that the top floors are almost touching. The area is immaculately clean and tidy, the streets swept, the house fronts gleaming with new paint and extravagant hanging baskets overflowing with flowers, so that the effect wildly overshoots the picturesque and crash-lands into the kitsch. It's hyper-real, like a film set. As they walk, the Grey Goose is coming out with a sort of running autobiographical commentary, which Geraint is only half listening to. He hears "when they posted me to Syria" and "the opposition had considerable assets in place" and he realises he's thinking Bullshit!*

This is bullshit! There's a problem that really intrigues him, and he concentrates on it to the point where the American's voice becomes a meaningless drone in his ear. It's this: which is actually the creepier and more sinister scenario – that he's being led around these dark and unfamiliar streets by an American Secret Service agent, or that he's being led around these dark and unfamiliar streets by someone who's pretending to be an American Secret Service agent? The question almost makes him laugh out loud, and he's just realised that this is the least depressed and lost and invisible he's felt in quite a long time, when they stop outside a massive black door, and the American presses a button set in the wall below a little speaker grille. The place doesn't look anything like a restaurant.

Geraint sipped at his coffee. He leaned back in the chair, stretching. He must have been smiling, because across the room the boy running the place smiled back at him, giving him a little wave. At the end of the row of computers to his right, Angela was frowning into her screen. He turned back to Janice's email.

There'll be another installment along soon. Now to my other project, pursuing and neutralising (or maybe neutering) the unsavoury Roddy and rescuing the beautiful Marina. This story is more melodramatic, and the characterisation less subtle, but what can you do? Anyway I'm meeting Roddy tomorrow, and I intend getting him to spill the beans. We're meeting at the White Hound, by the way. I haven't quite decided on an approach yet. I'm toying with the idea of full-on sex, beginning with incredibly plunging neckline and vamping it from there, although I'm not much endowed in the cleavage line, as you know, so perhaps I'll resort to violence instead. I'll email you tomorrow and let you know what happens. Please write to me old friend, I really want to know what's happening.

Angela left her seat and came over.

"Had an email from Mam," she said. "She loves her computer, Dad never touches it. Funny that, you'd think it would be the other way round." Geraint nodded. "Are you going to be long?" Angela asked him. "I want to go to the police station, tell them about this CIA man."

"Just let me reply to this," he said. "Why don't you get a coffee or something." She moved away, sighing.

You were right about Jessica, he wrote. Or at least, half right. Very pretty girl, they've obviously been seeing a lot of each other. But she doesn't know where he is, I mean, she says she doesn't, and I believe her. In a way, she doesn't really seem worried about him. She doesn't know what's happened to him, but she seems to feel that he's OK, that this is something he's chosen to do. And the really odd thing is I find that very reassuring. I know it doesn't make sense, but I do. I suppose she's the one that's been seeing him over these last couple of weeks, so maybe she knows things about him that we don't. Anyway, we've been to see the police, all the usual things, which we'll keep on doing. The past is still here, co-existing, occupying the same space as the present, Briggana's oratory is a beach-café. It sounds crazy but you may be right, it's all part of the same thing, as though I'll find Aled by looking for St Brygga, or find St Brygga by looking for Aled. You've got me worried about poor Geraint. Is it really closing in on him?

Detective Kazantsakis was out of his office, couldn't be contacted. They left a message for him: Angela wanted to see him tomorrow morning, it was urgent. The policeman at the desk nodded, making a note.

"*Ine epígon,*" he wrote. "Is urgent."

The shadows were starting to lengthen as they walked back towards the apartment building. Swifts and housemartins dipped under the eaves and through groves of eucalyptus.

"We're not getting anywhere," Angela said. "Nothing's happening. It's like a nightmare."

"We've only just got here," Geraint said. He watched his feet scuffing the dusty road on the edge of town, thinking of dark tarmac, and steel tread-plate on the moving walkways at the airport. "We've only been here a day."

"And we've got nowhere," Angela said. "We didn't even manage to tell the police about the CIA man."

"We will tomorrow," Geraint said. "Even though Jessica seems to think it was a joke."

"Jessica!" Angela said, scowling. "Let's all make sure we don't miss a single word of what Jessica has to say." Geraint glanced at her.

"She's seen him the most recently," he said. "That makes her better informed than us."

"Does it really?" Angela said. "That makes her better informed than me, does it? Better informed about Aled?"

"Better informed about what he's been doing in the last couple of weeks," Geraint said. "What he's been thinking about." They stepped to the side of the road as a tractor and trailer came past, blowing smoke, the driver tipping his hat to them, the trailer full of melons as bright as beach-balls. Angela waited while the noise wrapped itself around them and then faded away down the road.

"You're still on about that," she said. "You think he just buggered off for some reason, God knows what."

The scraping of the cicadas, hallucinatory, seemed to jump up in volume as though some excitement had run through them.

"I'm not saying that," Geraint said, raising his voice against the uproar. "It's a possibility, that's all."

"It's not a possibility," Angela said. "It's impossible. He would never do that to me. Don't you think I know him better than that?"

Mr Panagiotis was painting a window frame at the front of the building, dabbing on minute quantities of blue with a tiny brush. He turned to them, bowing, as they approached.

"*Kalispéra,*" Geraint said. "Could I ask you something? About my son, about Aled?"

Mr Panagiotis carefully put the brush down on the lid of the tin.

"Please," he said, "*Parakaló.*"

"Did my son talk about his work?" Geraint asked. "About tourism, about bringing visitors here?"

"Very nice boy," Mr Panagiotis said. "Everybody like."

"Did he see people here, did he talk to people here, people in the travel business?"

Mr Panagiotis nodded, smiling. "Talk to everybody," he said, "very friendly boy."

They looked at each other, nodding, smiling, baffled. Geraint sighed.

"I think we'll have to try this again, with Jessica," he said.

"I'm going to my room," Angela said.

It was dark by the time Jessica got back from teaching. Geraint had been dozing over the guidebook, drifting in and out of sleep. He knocked on Angela's door.

"Come and get something to eat," he said.

"I'm asleep. I'll see you in the morning."

The night was warm, softened by the breeze. On the water front the bars and cafés were lit, waiters shaking out paper tablecloths. Further round the curve of the bay, the lights of Corinth and Loutraki hung in glimmering strings. Across the Gulf, the eye of the light-house opened, looked away.

"We could go here, to *Platonos*," Jessica said. "Where we were last night. Unless you'd rather somewhere else."

Geraint took a deep breath. The smell of grilling meat, garlic and rosemary, hung in the air like incense.

"*Platonos* is fine," he said.

In the bay the lights of a fishing boat, heading for the harbour at Corinth, flickered on the water. Geraint sipped at his retsina.

"Aled sent me an email about this," he said. "That it tasted like wood varnish. He was right."

"He got used to it," Jessica said, smiling. "It grows on you."

Geraint looked at her across the remains of the meal.

"Tell me about him," he said. "How he spent his time, what he was thinking about." In the silence, he became aware of booming voices and bursts of music from the open-air cinema a block away behind the café.

"It was as though he'd let himself off the lead," Jessica said slowly. "He had a joke about it, something about a dog jumping in the river. I don't mean staying up all night, or drinking too much. He did a bit of that, of course." She shook her head, smiling to herself. "It was more like he was seeing things he hadn't let himself see before." She made a vague gesture out across the bay. "The way the past is so strong here, the way you can feel it, just below the surface, as though time was transparent."

"I feel the same thing," Geraint said. "It's just I can't quite imagine Aled talking like that." He smiled, seeing him. "He's never been interested in the Museum, in archaeology. I think of him as, you

115

know, practical, level-headed. Not like me."

"Maybe that's just one side to him," Jessica said. "Maybe that's the side he felt he had to show people, until he came here." She looked up at him. "I expect that's the side Angela sees."

Geraint nodded. "Perhaps," he said.

"Anyway, the first couple of times I met him he was a bit like that; he was on about his work, the travel agency, all the business he was going to do here."

The waiter came to the table and started collecting their plates. "But then he seemed to lose interest. He stopped talking about it, anyway. He wanted to learn about this place, he was so enthusiastic. We went to Asprolimáni." She pointed across the bay. "To the sanctuary, below the light-house there. We went to the Citadel on Acrocorinth. We went to Ancient Corinth two or three times. Did I say, he thought he'd found something, to do with your saint there, in the Museum."

"I thought he was just humouring me. I'm amazed," Geraint said. "He always called her St Bugger. I never thought he was interested."

"I meant to show you this," Jessica said. She took an envelope out of her pocket, drawing out a folded sheet of paper and passing it across to him. It was a note, in Aled's handwriting:

I really want to see islands with you, Sifnos, Serifos, they're such beautiful names. But I'm running out of time. I don't know what to do. See you tonite. A

"I thought you ought to see it," Jessica said.

"When did he write you this?" Geraint asked. She shrugged.

"In his second week some time, not sure what day. He dropped it off at the school for me. Can I have it back please?"

For a moment it was as if Aled was at the table with them, breaking bread, haloed in the hanging lantern-light. Beyond the brightly lit café and the busy water-front street, the dark sea suggested itself, unlit, an absence.

"Are you alright?" Jessica was asking him. He nodded, clearing his throat.

"I'd like to see some of these places tomorrow," he said. "I'd like to go to the Museum."

116

Chapter Eleven

They had to wait nearly half an hour before detective Kazantsakis could see them. He was affable but distracted.

"So, people, what can I do for you today? What's new?" He glanced at his watch. Angela began to tell him about the Grey Goose. He whistled through his teeth. "The CIA," he said. "Is that right."

"I think it might be partly a joke," Geraint said.

"Partly?"

"A sort of a guess, then."

Angela glared at him. "They thought he was suspicious," she said. "They said he was sinister." She turned to the detective. "He obviously needs looking into. You need to talk to that Jessica, see what she knows, maybe she'll be a bit more straighforward with you."

An ambiguous communication passed momentarily between Kazantsakis and Geraint. The Greek wrote something in his notebook. He nodded.

"That's good," he said. "I'll do that. I'll drop in at *Korintho-net* also, have a chat with the kids there."

Geraint and Angela crossed the square in front of the police station, under the Archbishop's outspread arms, into the deep shade of a palm tree.

"Elaine won't be here until late afternoon," Geraint said. "Maybe later if she's a long time at the Consulate." Angela drew a deep breath.

"It'll be so nice to see her," she said. "I can't wait."

Geraint looked at his watch. "I'm meeting Jessica at ten thirty," he said. "She's taking me to Ancient Corinth. I want to see the Museum there. Do you want to come?" Angela stared at him.

"I'm really not in the mood for sightseeing right now," she said. "I hope you have an enjoyable time."

He had a coffee while he waited for Jessica, sitting at a table set back from the road. The street was busy, high-school kids skipping through the traffic. Buses drew up outside the café, the automatic doors clapping open. Geraint deciphered the destinations mounted on signs above the driver on the tinted windscreens: *Megara, Aghos Theodori, Loutraki, Egira.*

There was a hand-bill pasted to the glass front of the café, and he moved his chair round to look at it. A girl's face looked back at him, another lost child. *MISSING*, Geraint read. *EXAFANISE. CAN YOU HELP.* A dark, rather severe face, the expression self-contained, thoughtful. Fourteen years old, missing nearly two months. There was a phone number to call, and an email address.

He saw Jessica without recognising her for a moment, watching a pretty girl dodge through the traffic, waving thanks as a car stopped for her, a moment of distance which set him wondering about her, about her relationship with Aled, about what she wanted, what she knew. He found himself glancing at her as they settled into their seats on the bus. Angela's hostility to the girl was perhaps as inevitable and autonomic as a reflex, but he realised that his own reaction had been just as instinctive, an unreflective accepting of everything she had told him.

"Are you alright?" Jessica asked him. "Has there been any news?" He shook his head.

Ancient Corinth was bigger than his reading had prepared him for, a disordered expanse of tumbled masonry, piles of shaped stone, circular column bases, stretching over many hectares. At various points the ruins were more intact, sections of wall head-high, flagged courtyards, arches, shallow flights of broken steps. The site was bounded at one end by the columns of the Temple of Apollo, at the other by the sheer brow of Acrocorinth and the Citadel, and it was fringed around its perimeter by the shade of cypresses and pine trees, but the central area of ruins lay open and desolate, bleached in the crushing heat. Geraint tried to imagine Aled here.

"We came later in the day," Jessica said, "when the shadows are longer."

Crossing the flagstones of the market place in the bewildering intensity of light and the uproar of the cicadas, they found the pulpit where St Paul had delivered his peevish, unwelcome and dogmatic message to the Corinthians. *It is good for a man not to touch a woman*, he had told them. On a wall a lizard hung as if it had been stencilled there. *It is good for them if they abide even as I. But if they cannot contain, let them marry; for it is better to marry than to burn.* Geraint glanced up at the shocking rise of the Acrocorinth, the sheer face lit with a dull glow. He thought of the cool recesses of the Temple of Aphrodite deep in the Citadel, the sheen of marble.

"We went up there," Jessica said, intercepting his glance. "He said you'd told him about the slaves of the Temple. We climbed the whole way on foot. He said: *It's a long way to go for a shag.*"

"What about the Sanctuary, half way up?" Geraint asked. "The Sanctuary of Necessity and Violence?"

Jessica shook her head. "I don't remember him talking about that," she said.

The Museum was set in a grove of cypress, down a flight of steps into a long hall lit by roof-lights and lined by statues and fragments of sculpture, Greek and Roman torsos, a horse's head, a solitary foot in a sandal. There was a display case of votive offerings to Asklepios, little crude terracotta charms and amulets in the shape of breasts, hands, lips, penises: *the lineaments of gratified desire.* They passed the marble heads of children, their features blurred into sleepiness by time, a head of Aphrodite with soporific eyes, Caesar's austere, immediately recognisable face, a girl's body, pliant, wreathed in a flowing sheath of stone.

More than the heads, Geraint thought, it was the torsos, male or female, sinuous, soft or muscled, that most expressed the human over time. The disruptions of history had stripped off limbs, heads, leaving this essence, this persistent vessel. And everywhere, at your feet, under your hands, this fabulous texture of the marble, these beautiful, creamy, flesh-like tones and surfaces, lit by glittering highlights, like sweat, like stars, like points of love, as though the marble sweated light.

The material is so magical, he thought, so silky, perhaps especially when the perfect sheen has been eroded off, or not yet achieved in unfinished work. You sense the flesh of the stone, its weight and life, its enigmatic sexuality.

Geraint shook his head.

"It's hard for me to imagine Aled here," he said. "It's just not how I think of him, like you were describing someone else."

"I don't mean he was deadly serious," Jessica said. "You know that, everything is a laugh with Aled. Like he loved this, come and see."

She gestured him over to a painted amphora, decorated with the dark silhouette of a frantically running naked athlete, bug-eyed with effort, enormous straining thighs and buttocks, scything arms and legs, ludicrous little erect cock.

Geraint smiled. "I hadn't thought about the sporting connection," he said. "There were really important games at Corinth, massive, almost as big as Olympia."

"And the little offerings," Jessica said. "The little boobs and bits, he thought they were brilliant." Geraint nodded.

"I can imagine," he said. "It was picturing him as a serious academic all of a sudden that was giving me the problem."

The hall opened onto a cloister, lined with fragments of memorial sculpture, carved inscriptions in angular, unpunctuated script. Geraint stooped to look more closely.

"*DIS MANIBUS,*" he read. "To the spirits of the departed. Eumachia, Public Priestess." He straightened up. "She paid for an altar to be built here," he said. "It was dedicated to Pity."

Voices and the shuffle of feet drifted down from the other end of the hall as a coach party arrived. They could hear the tour guide raising her voice in a precise, practised, carrying monotone: *des objets funèbres, d'origine romaine.*

"Here's something about Justinian," Geraint said. "He was Emperor when Briggana was here." He squatted down to have a closer look. "*Lumen de lumine deus verus,*" he read. "Light of light, true God."

The inscription was on a marble plaque, a corner broken off but most of the remaining lettering surprisingly sharp. Geraint ran his fingers over the incised grooves; perhaps it had been protected by having been covered up, buried in an earthquake. He concentrated on trying to translate it, locating the verbs, rearranging the word order, murmuring.

> *Light of light, true God of true God, guard the emperor justinian and his servant the holy riggana along with… who live in greece… according to God.*

The word or part-word *riggana* was at the edge of the break in the stone, following the trace of a cursive stroke that could have been part of the letter B.

"Now I've really found you," Geraint said. "Here you are at last."

Jessica had come over and stood at his shoulder as he crouched in front of the inscription.

"Do you think this is what Aled saw?" he said, looking up at her. "His amazing discovery?"

In that case he must be standing exactly where Aled had stood, eight or ten days ago, looking through his eyes at an artefact that Briggana herself might have seen, might have touched. He had found them both. The three of them were reunited, he thought, aware of the thudding of his heart. They were together, but of course only in place, separated by veils of time, a medium experienced as fluid but which hardens into an opacity as impenetrable after a few hours or days as after fifteen hundred years. Only memory can see through time, move in it with open eyes. Without memory we can only circle endlessly round the present moment. This is why the lost are lost, he thought; why the missing stay missing.

In his pocket his phone trilled an alert, a text from Elaine.

> *Just got in Athens bloody hot. Going straight to the consulate. Assume no progress today since heard nothing.*

⭑ ⭑ ⭑

At the bus station, the missing girl's poster had been defaced with a red marker pen, giving her a beard and a moustache. He ordered a coffee and texted Elaine:

Ask for the final Corinth stop – Stathmós leoforíon Korinthos. Will be in café opposite where buses pull in.

He thought about the inscription in the Museum cloister. After Jessica left he had gone back to look at it again, taking a photograph and copying the lettering into his notebook. The Briggana he had found was not quite the one he had been looking for. The marble tablet suggested status, followers. But perhaps it was precisely her poverty and asceticism, the personal obscurity he had always imagined for her, that drew people to her, just as pilgrims had gathered at the foot of the pillar where Simeon Stylites crouched for forty years, dressed in rags and all but embalmed by the desert sun, fifteen metres above them. On the way out, he passed a marble bas-relief of Icarus, falling into the sea, falling like a stone dropped in the well of the sky, falling forever, another lost child.

Elaine was very blonde, her hair thick and fashionably tangled, butter-coloured, streaked with darker shades of amber.

"You're looking terrific," Geraint said. She gave him a short, impatient glare.

"I'm sick of towing this suitcase around," she said. "And I'm not getting on any more buses or trains. There must be a cab-rank somewhere."

The town was coming to life again as the afternoon lengthened hazily. They found taxis in the square behind the bus station.

"Are you alright sharing the apartment with Angela?" Geraint asked. Elaine shrugged, closing her eyes and leaning back in the seat.

"Anything so long as I can get in the shower," she said.

The traffic had come to a standstill, the road blocked as far ahead as they could see, the air torpid with exhaust fumes. "The Consulate was a bloody waste of time," Elaine said. "Not what the Foreign Office told me at all."

"They know about him, don't they?" Geraint asked. "They must have had the details through by now."

Elaine sighed.

"I'll tell you about it," she said. "I need a shower first, and a drink."

The driver twisted round and said something to them, then swung

122

through a right, down a cobbled side street. At a pavement café a group of old men were playing backgammon. A pick-up truck blocked the way, backing into a gateway. The taxi driver strummed his fingers on the steering wheel, murmuring in a droning monotone. Elaine looked out of the window, shaking her head.

"What in the world was Aled doing here?" she said. "What possessed him to come here?"

At the apartment building, Geraint watched her beguile Mr Panagiotis with weary ease, her touch light, practised.

"I am so pleased," Mr Panagiotis said softly. "I am so sorry." He told them that Miss Angela had gone for a walk, perhaps along the beach. "Where is Jessica?" he said, shrugging extravagantly. "I don't know."

Geraint made highballs with his duty free, and he and Elaine sat in wicker chairs on the balcony, watching the restless sea running up the shingle.

"In different circumstances this would be quite pleasant," Elaine said, closing her eyes, turning her face to the sun. Geraint nodded, watching the light in her hair.

"Tell me about the Consulate," he said. "What happened?"

"I don't think they were expecting me at all," Elaine said. "No sign of the Vice Consul, anyway." She sat forward, sipped her drink. "I went through security, found myself in this waiting room, dozens of gloomy Albanians asking about visas. Sounds chaotic, but it was just dispiriting, everybody talking in whispers. The dead hand of apathetic bureaucracy, a place where dreams die." She laughed briefly. "Eventually I got buzzed in. You sit in this tiny booth facing a glass wall. On the other side a woman appears, and talks to you through a little grille." Elaine sipped at her drink, shaking her head. "Anyway, they didn't tell me anything I hadn't already been told by the missing persons helpline. Said they didn't really get involved with this sort of thing. Said it was between the police at home and the local police here. Inter-agency cooperation." She looked at Geraint.

"So here I am," she said. "Now, tell me everything you've been doing."

The mountains across the bay dissolved in the deepening haze. From time to time Mr Panagiotis appeared, bringing up another wicker chair, closing a sun umbrella, glancing shyly at Elaine as he passed.

"I'm not trying to duplicate what you've been doing," Elaine was saying.

"I need to see the police for myself, that's all. For God's sake, Geraint, I'm his mother." She shivered, getting to her feet. "I need to put something else on."

Geraint sat in the gathering dark, listening to the clatter of her footsteps on the concrete stair. From the bamboos, a cicada started up, a few preparatory scrapes and rasps leading into the fully articulated song. He heard the scrape of the front door.

"You have no idea what it's been like," Angela was saying, as she and Elaine appeared at the top of the stairs.

At *Platonos* the waiter greeted them, leading them over to the table where Geraint had sat with Jessica the night before, drawing up more chairs, spreading out a fresh table cloth with a sweep and flourish.

"So Angela and I will go to the police station tomorrow," Elaine said. She reached for the jug of wine and poured three glasses. "Let's drink to success," she said. "We're a team now." She took a sip of wine, wrinkling her nose and holding the glass up to the light. "I've also been thinking about a private investigator," she said. "I've got a couple of addresses, one in Athens, one here. We'll see. We'll get a feel for how competent the local police are."

She clinked glasses with Angela. Geraint watched the two of them across the table. Angela had pulled her chair round close to Elaine's and was leaning towards her.

"I'm so glad you're here," she said. Elaine nodded, glancing at Geraint.

"Me too," she said. She pinched the bridge of her nose between her fingers for a moment, screwing her eyes shut. "God, it's been hectic recently. It was tough to get away." She looked round the restaurant. "Like I said, in any other circumstances this would make a nice change." Watching her, Geraint thought that really, for all the bitterness it had generated, that whole affair of hers had been a pretext, an irrelevancy. Elaine's significant other had always been London, the city itself: black cabs and red buses, conferences and restaurants, tall buildings, the leaping span of bridges crossing the Thames, aeroplanes coming in to Heathrow. Even in happy times, their happiest times had been in London. Their mistake, elaborated over many years, had been to think she could be happy anywhere else. She looked across at Geraint. "Explain about this inscription again," she said. "I don't quite get what you're trying to tell me."

"Firstly, it means I was right about St Brygga," he said. "This is where she built her oratory."

Angela pulled a face.

"He's been like this since we got here," she said, turning to Elaine. "The shrine of this and the shrine of that. The temple of whatsisname."

"It's his job, dear," Elaine said. "It's what he does for a living. And we are in Greece, after all. You have to expect temples." She turned back to Geraint. "What's it got to do with Aled, though? That's what I don't understand."

"Exactly," Angela said. "What's it got to do with Aled?"

The waiter set down plates of food, making space on the table.

"Kalí órexi," he said. "Bon appetit."

"It's always the same," Angela said, shaking her head. "Salad, feta, bloody olives. We've eaten the same food every meal."

"Aled told me he'd discovered something about Briggana," Geraint said. "He mentioned it in an email, and Jessica said the same thing."

"He never mentioned it to me," Angela said.

"I think the inscription is what he found," Geraint said. "That was his discovery."

"Does it help us find Aled?" Elaine asked. Angela shook her head vigorously.

"I think it might," Geraint said. "That's the whole point. Perhaps it's possible for us to follow in his footsteps."

"He's been on and on like this," Angela said to Elaine. "Can you imagine how it makes me feel?"

"Retrace whatever journey he's set off on," Geraint said.

"You see?" Angela said, her voice rising. "You see what I mean?"

"Which raises the possibility of catching up with him," Geraint said.

Elaine pushed at a slice of tomato with her fork, a trail of golden oil following it across the plate.

"I can't quite see this in connection with Aled," she said. "Latin inscriptions, and Celtic saints. It's not really him, is it?" She looked up at Geraint. "It doesn't really sound like him."

"You see?" Angela said to Geraint. "That's exactly what I said to you."

Geraint drank some wine and refilled his glass.

"I know," he said. "I agree with you. But we never saw him here, did we? We never saw him here in Greece."

"Are you saying I don't really know him?" Angela said. "I never really knew him? Is that what you're saying?"

Looking up, Geraint saw Jessica on the other side of the terrace. She was talking to the waiter, who at that moment pointed across to their table.

"Jessica," Geraint called out. "Over here."

"Bloody hell!" Angela whispered in a fierce hiss to Elaine. "She hangs around us all the time. Every bloody minute."

"Come and join us," Geraint said. He waved at the waiter. "Let's get more wine." He moved his chair to make room. "You haven't eaten?" Jessica shook her head, smiling.

"Elaine," Geraint said. "This is Jessica I told you about. This is Aled's mother."

The Greek family from the rooms next door at the apartment building had taken the table next to them and waved. The place was full. A teenage girl had joined the waiter, skipping between tables serving food. The air was scented with woodsmoke, cinnamon, rosemary. Bouzouki music was playing somewhere out the back.

"There were one or two places he particularly liked," Jessica was saying to Elaine. "Places he said were really magical."

"Can you speak up a bit," Elaine said. She looked around the bustling terrace appreciatively. "They don't believe in talking in whispers here, do they."

"I don't think I've ever hated anywhere as much as I hate this place," Angela said.

"The Sanctuary at Asprolimáni," Jessica said, "the sunken harbour at Cenchrea. Places where the past rises to the surface: doorways."

"Doorways," Angela said. "What do you mean doorways?" She turned to Elaine. "Do you have the slightest idea what she's talking about?"

Elaine put her hand on Angela's arm.

"Hold on a minute," she said.

"I had a conversation with Janice about this," Geraint said. "Before we came here, the notion of liminality." Angela stared at him.

"What are you talking about?" she said.

"The idea of portals," Geraint said. "There are moments in your life which you can think of as doorways. You turn through them and you're never the same again."

"What is this crap?" Angela said. She poured herself a glass of wine.

"I remember Janice describing it," Geraint said. "You'd be walking down the street, and on your right you'd see an archway that you'd somehow never noticed before, and you'd turn through it, without thinking." He caught Elaine's eye. "And there would be no way back," he said. "And nothing would ever be the same again."

A group of teenage girls came over to their table and surrounded Jessica, cooing. She smiled at them, trying to disengage, saying something to them in Greek, and then in English:

"I'll see you in class tomorrow. You were very good today, I was very proud of you."

"It's an approach," Geraint said quietly to Elaine. "Of course we look for him in other ways: the police, maybe like you said, private investigators. But when I stood in that cloister looking at the inscription, you have no idea how close he felt. It was like I was just a few steps behind him. I have to follow that." Elaine shook her head, looking into his eyes.

"I don't know," she said. "Why isn't all of this just you, telling yourself a comforting story, making yourself feel better?"

"I can't believe any of you," Angela said. Jessica's students looked over at her, startled by the tone of her voice. They moved away, whispering. "You're behaving like this is some sort of game. I feel like I'm in a nightmare. I feel like I'm screaming and nobody can hear me, like that fucking picture, that scream picture. You just smile, as if I wasn't here, like I didn't exist." She had a piece of bread in her hands and was tearing it into pieces. "Aled's gone," she said. "He's disappeared, and you sit here talking about doorways. Nothing's happening." Elaine put her arm round her. "I'm completely alone here," Angela said. "You treat me like I'm invisible."

"No you're not," Elaine said. "And you're right, all this theorizing is no good." She looked across at Geraint. She reached for her handbag, drawing out a folded sheet of paper. "They made this up for me at the missing persons helpline," she said bleakly. "I've got it on a memory stick, need to find a printshop or an internet café, get a few dozen printed up."

She unfolded the paper and smoothed it out on the table, a handbill, broad stripes of bright red, white lettering framing a photograph:

MISSING – HAVE YOU SEEN HIM? – CAN YOU HELP?

Aled's face looked out at them.

★ ★ ★

The waiter called after them as they left.

"Kaliníchta," he said, "Good night. Sto kaló."

"Sto kaló," Geraint repeated softly, walking beside Elaine. "It means: Into the good," he said. "Isn't it a beautiful phrase. It's a benediction, a valedictory: Go into the good."

"Christ, you get on my nerves sometimes," Elaine said.

Chapter Twelve

From the lighthouse, Liminidhi was no more than a pale stubble along the margin where land and sea meet. Along that fringe below the mountains, tiny grapes were sweetening on the vine, old men drank coffee and read the newspaper, traffic idled boiling in the streets. Some mirrored surface caught the sun for a moment in a flash of intense light. Geraint imagined Elaine and Angela on their way to the police station, the town dropping away below them through vineyards and orchards, the horizon of mountains stepping down to the headland on which he and Jessica were now standing. He had a strange sense of inversion at the foot of the anomalous white tower, looking out as though through the eye of the lighthouse.

"Like looking out of someone else's eyes," he said, "at yourself."

Jessica looked round, missing her footing for a moment on the steep path. Below them, beyond a grove of stunted pine trees, the Sanctuary of Hera revealed itself, a series of terraces stepping down to a harbour at the lip of the sea.

"Aled said he wanted to come here by boat," Jessica said. "Get a fisherman to bring him across from Liminidhi, tie up down there." She pointed to the stone mole that ran out into the water, protecting the landfall, and Geraint saw him for a moment, stepping up onto the quay, the fishing boat below him on the bright water. Someone would throw a bag up to him, and he would lean down, offering his hand to them, helping them out of the boat. He glanced at Jessica.

"And did he?" he asked. She shook her head.

"Not with me, anyway."

The breeze was blowing off the sea, shattering the surface into dazzling points of light. Above them, the Sanctuary lay in the bowl of a short, steep-sided valley at the sea's edge, lined by arcades of broken columns, broad flights of steps.

"This place was ancient when Briggana was here," he said. "It would have been intact, and maybe still in use, at least furtively. Maybe she saw firelight across the bay, flickering on the water. They were still carrying out purges of non-Christians in Justinian's reign; they were banned from public office. If you were Christian and lapsed from the True Faith, you could be executed." He looked back across the bay in the direction of Liminidhi, thinking of his Saint on the beach, staring across the water, hot-eyed, outraged, drawing down curses on the pagans. "People must have gone back," he said. "They must have wanted to go back to the old religions if you had to threaten them with death to stop them. I bet they were still coming here to worship Hera while the Christians were wrangling over heresies in Corinth."

They watched the water lapping gently at the stone quay for a few moments, then walked up into the Sanctuary. Geraint ran his fingers over the fluted surface of a column. "This must have been a brilliant site to work on," he said. "They excavated it in the Thirties, British archaeologists, there was almost nothing here, barely a trace. Imagine turning all this stuff up, out here, in the middle of nowhere. Brought their gear in on donkeys, lived in tents. And here it was, the real thing: the past, just under your feet, waiting to be released, like a statue in a block of stone." They walked up a set of steps to the next terrace, the flagstones worn to a powdery smoothness. "You work from hints, and guesses, and fragments of text. You think: *There is a message here. I am being told something.* You lay out the line of a trench and you dig, maybe for days. At night you cook over an open fire, watching the shooting stars. In the hottest part of the day you swim, and keep out of the sun. Then suddenly one day the shovel rings on solid stone and it's there, not quite where you expected, running away obliquely from where you'd marked it on your plan, but it's really there. You've reached across a couple of thousand years and you've found it!"

He smiled to himself, thinking of Llanfrychan, and the County Museum, and Janice, chain-smoking in the Social History store. Standing in this circle of light with the sea all around him, and thinking about the long obscurity of the road that had brought him here, he pictured Aled standing in this same place, a few days ago. Aled would have been looking forwards, not backwards. The reveries this place inspired would have been of the future, not the past, of freedom, not constraint; of endless possibility. He looked at Jessica.

"Tell me what he talked about," he said. "When you were here, what did you talk about?"

"We talked about the future," she said. "About setting out on a journey, about not knowing what's going to happen next."

"Like the note he sent you," Geraint said.

"This place is all about leaving," she said. "Don't you think? Setting sail in the evening." She looked out to sea.

"Why leaving?" Geraint asked. Jessica looked at him.

"Maybe arriving too," she said. "Journeys, anyway. We talked about that, how you just want to get up and go. That was a really strong feeling: when we went to the sunken harbour, the other side of Corinth; the stone piers running out into the sea, just below the waves. Maybe it's because of all the islands, all the islands out there, just over the horizon. He said that islands are points on a journey. Islands are places you leave from, or arrive at, aren't they? You don't stay."

"I suppose you can be shipwrecked or imprisoned; maybe bewitched," Geraint said. Jessica nodded.

"Until you're rescued," she said.

★ ★ ★

Elaine was on the terrace when Geraint got back to the apartment. She didn't hear him as he came up the steps, and he stood and watched her for a moment. She was sitting very still, staring out to sea. She turned as he brought over another chair to the little table. Her eyes were shadowed, set in a map of fine lines he hadn't been aware of before.

"You look shattered," he said, and she nodded, putting her sunglasses back on.

"Hell of a day," she said. Preceded by a faint, silvery tinkling, Mr Panagiotis appeared at the top of the steps, carrying a tray. He came over to the table and set out a small bottle of ouzo, a jug of water, a bowl of ice and several little dishes of food. Elaine looked up at him, shading her eyes against the low sun, smiling. "You're very kind," she said.

Mr Panagiotis murmured something and hurried away. "I only asked for a glass of water," Elaine said. "Tell me what you did today."

"I will," Geraint said. "How did you get on with the police?"

Mr Panagiotis reappeared, setting down a second glass on the table with an apologetic shrug towards Geraint. He gestured at the food.

"Mezédhes," he said, "to eat, please."

"Angela's gone to lie down," Elaine said. "She's not really coping, you know. You have to be nice to her." Geraint nodded. "Means I have to put on a good front," she said. "Maybe that's a good thing, keeps me focused." She drew a short breath. "I saw the detective," she said. "The fat one, the young one. What was his name?"

"Kazantsakis," Geraint said. "Nick. Is he fat?"

Elaine nodded.

"Nick," she said. "It's hard to tell. They follow procedures. They're professionals. You don't get personal commitment, you have no sense of how hard they're going to try."

"So long as you get professional commitment," Geraint said.

"So you feel like a number," Elaine said. "You feel like your son has become a statistic." Geraint poured the ouzo, dropping ice into the glasses, watching as the liquid turned blind and milky. "Which he has," Elaine said. "He kept asking me about mental problems, did he have any mental illness? Apparently that's why they're so interested in the clothes people were last seen wearing: people with mental illness don't change their clothes. You learn something every day." She sipped at the drink, shivered. "Anyway, they're faxing off the missing poster. It'll go to every police station in Greece, so he says. And they printed out a hundred copies. I brought twenty five back with me, we'll put them up around here." They looked at each other. "Might jog someone's memory," Elaine said. "He could be ill somewhere. He could have had a breakdown, or lost his memory. He could be wandering around." She prodded at a piece of octopus tentacle with a cocktail stick. "I think this is probably the most ghastly situation I've ever been in."

"He wrote a note to Jessica," Geraint said. "She showed it to me the other night. It was about wanting to go to the islands with her. He said: *I'm running out of time. I don't know what to do.*"

"The other night?" Elaine said. "Why did you wait to tell me?"

"I never had a chance," Geraint said. "I didn't want to bring it up while Angela was around." He sipped his drink. "I thought about the note today," he said. "She was talking about conversations she'd had with him, about journeys, about setting off into the unknown. He had a theory about islands, how they trigger off journeys, that liminality thing, I suppose. It was when we were at the Sanctuary, out there." He looked across the bay. "It was very strange being over there, looking back here. Like the wrong end of a telescope."

"Tell me about the note," Elaine said.

"It's a beautiful place," Geraint said. "A really magical place."

"Tell me about the bloody note."

"She said he'd dropped it in at the language school, the second week he was here. It was about wanting to go to some islands with her. There were a couple of names, I don't remember what they were. He said: *I'm running out of time, I don't know what to do.*"

"How much use is that without the names of the islands?" Elaine said. "They could be really important. How can you not remember the names? What did you actually do today? What did you do all day while we were sweating it out in Corinth?"

"Jessica still has the note," Geraint said. "They both began with *S.*"

"This is exactly the way I remember conversations with you," Elaine said.

"If I looked on a map I'd probably recognise them," Geraint said. He sipped at the ouzo, thinking about Aled's email: toothpaste, and wood varnish. "When she talks about him, you think: *perhaps I never understood him properly, perhaps I barely know him.*"

"Unless it's all bullshit," Elaine said.

"I don't think so," Geraint said. He shook his head. "As far as I can see, they spent practically every minute of the two weeks together."

"How does that help us?" Elaine said. "How exactly does that help us?" She looked at him. "How can you be like this? It's just bouncing off you, isn't it?"

"No it isn't," Geraint said. "I want to find him, you know that."

"After the police station we went to the private investigator's

133

office," Elaine said. "*Aristotle Enquiries*. The website said they had offices in New York and London. I never had time to check out the London office, but the Corinth branch is pretty seedy, let me tell you." She sighed, shaking her head. "They didn't even speak much English, but I left some posters with them, and they're on the case. We'll pay them for a couple of weeks, see what happens. There's a possibility that they'll come up with something. There's a possibility." She got up and walked to the edge of the terrace, looking out at the headland. The pale evening blink of the lighthouse was just visible against the fading glow of the sky. "What are you achieving with your visits to sanctuaries, and museums?" she said, without looking round at him. "You're just displacing your anxieties, aren't you?"

"I can't say this in front of Angela," Geraint said. "But this is what I think: I think that coming here turned his world upside down. I think he's probably in love with Jessica, but in any case I think he realised he just couldn't go back, settle for the travel agency, settle for Angela."

"Where are you getting this from?" Elaine said. "What evidence have you got?"

"Talking to Jessica," Geraint said. "Hearing what they talked about, what he was thinking about."

"If it's true."

"Why would she make it up?"

Elaine turned to face him. "Do you really think he'd do that?" she said. "Just disappear without a word? Not telling anyone?"

"That's the whole point," Geraint said. "Maybe he has told us. Maybe he's given us the information, but we're not looking in the right place. When I saw that inscription in the Museum, it felt like a message from him. That's why we went to the Sanctuary today. That's why I want to go to the sunken harbour. I want to go to the places that Jessica says meant a lot to him. If he's left a message for us I want to find it."

Elaine shook her head, looking at him with a kind of sadness.

"Must be very comforting to believe that," she said.

"I only believe it some of the time," Geraint said. "Other times I wake up in the middle of the night, same as you do. It's a possibility, that's all, like your private detectives."

"Looking at the stuff he left behind, I was sure there'd be something, some message," she said. "I spent so long going through it, but there was nothing. *Love is making me thin, Love is making me think.* What does that mean?"

Geraint shrugged.

"Not what Angela thinks it means," he said.

"At least you could try to be practical," Elaine said, after a silence. "We need to talk to the ferry companies, or get the police to do that, get them to look through passenger lists. As soon as Jessica gets back we can find out what islands he was talking about, see if we can pick up a trace. Maybe I'll talk to the Aristotle place, as well as the police. Where would you get a ferry from?"

"Athens, I think," Geraint said. "Piraeus."

"Well then," Elaine said. "We need posters there for a start." She came back to the table and ate an olive, pursing her lips and blowing the pit out over the balustrade. "I want to talk to Jessica myself. I'm not relying on your version of what she says."

Geraint got to his feet.

"I'm going to walk up into town," he said. "Check my email. Feel like a stroll?" Elaine shook her head.

"I'll stay here. I'll see how Angela is. And talk to Jessica when she gets back."

In Liminidhi the shops were open for the evening session, and the bars and tavernas were busy. Light was spilling out onto the street from the bright interiors of a patisserie, a pool-hall where a group of teenagers posed with careful elegance around the tables. The red neon sign above *Korintho-Net* was buzzing and flickering in bursts of jittery morse code.

Dear Geraint, I hope you're getting answers but I won't ask because I know you'll tell me when there's any news. Do you want to hear how I got on with Roddy? I hope it doesn't sound too far-away and stupid and trivial. Anyway, you'll be glad to know I decided against the cleavage approach. I made sure I was three quarters of an hour late, although I phoned him half way through to say I was on my way in case he buggered off, so he was good and jumpy by the time I got there. Place was pretty empty, we sat across a little round table from each other, and I gave him my best amused-pitying-contemptuous look for at least a minute while we eye-balled each other over the top of our drinks. Once he was properly writhing, I put my pint down on the table. "Listen Roddy," I said, "you do realise that all this ferreting about you've been doing has attracted rather a lot of attention." "What do you mean?" he said. "What do you mean by that?" "Don't you realise," I said, "that you're under investigation yourself now? You've put yourself in the frame. You must have expected that to happen." It was so great, you should have seen him. "In the frame?" he said. "What's that supposed to mean? Who's investigating me?" I said, "Let's not play games Roddy, I think we both know the answer to that," – corny, I know, but irresistible. He looked like someone hearing voices in his head, like the fillings in his teeth were picking up a radio signal. "You've been annoying some rather powerful people, Roddy." I said. "I thought you'd know your way around better than to do that." It was a beautiful moment, it really was. I felt absolutely inspired. "It's time to think in terms of damage limitation," I said. I think the more outrageously corny I was, the more overwhelmed he got – stock phrases have a familiarity that seems to totally convince some people, the authority of the cliché. "It's time you and I put our heads together," I said, "see if there's any way out of this mess you're in."

"Why am I in a mess?" he said. "What have I done?" "Don't play dumb with me Roddy," I told him. I was having so much fun I had to stop myself from doing my Bogart: "Listen, shweetheart..." Anyway, I better cut to the chase. I told him that the only way I might be able to help him was if he levelled with me, told me everything he knew. I never really thought he'd go for it, I thought he'd see right through it, laugh in my face, but he was shaking, poor bugger. I think he really had been toying with the idea of blackmail; he was so easy to frighten off, he must have felt he was on very thin ice. I bought him a brandy ("drink it all down Roddy, you look like you need it"), and this is what I got: After Lewis died in the horse thing, old Mrs Ellis's will left Morton to the two daughters, Marina's mother Ffion, and her older sister Rosemary. According to Roddy there was a scandal with Rosemary, she got pregnant with some unsuitable person, had an abortion, and then flipped out, had a break-down. She took off, disappeared, no one

knew where she'd gone. Big police search, all that, not a trace. Ffion gets married, they live at Morton, husband dies, years go by. Then something very odd happened, I guess I was getting over-confident, or careless or something. I said "Go on." and Roddy looked at me, and I could see it click, I could see the precise moment. "You're having me on, aren't you?" he said, with a truly horrible little grin. I thought: fuck, I shouldn't have bought you that brandy, you little weasel, I should have kept you jittery. "You don't know anything, do you?" he said. "All that threat stuff, that was rubbish, wasn't it? You got nothing on me. You got no powerful friends." We looked at each other for a moment and I was trying my amused condescension thing but I could tell it wasn't working. "I'll tell you the best thing," he said. "What I just told you, that's pretty well public knowledge. I haven't told you the good stuff. It's what happened after that's interesting, and you're none the wiser about that, are you?" I said, "I wouldn't count on that Roddy," but I was losing it, it just wasn't working, and he knew it too. So I'm afraid I rather blew it Geraint. I think I can guess some of it, but it's not the same as dragging a confession out of the little creep, that's what I wanted and I really thought I'd done it. Still, it was fun in its way. I'll think of a different approach next time.

The kid on the till brought Geraint a coffee.

"Where is Jessica?" he said, "and your other friend, so beautiful."

Geraint smiled, taking the little cup, thanking him. There was an email from Lydia:

I am praying for you. I light a candle in Cardiff for your son.

He sipped the sweet coffee and wrote a reply to Janice.

I'm in the internet café on the main street, and there's people walking by outside, couples and families and groups of kids, I'm watching them through the glass shop-front, and some of them glance back at me, or maybe they're looking at the poster which I saw as I came in, stuck on the glass just to my right. It's a missing persons poster, and there's a picture of Aled on it. You can't imagine what it feels like to see it there.

He logged off.

To the east, the lights of Corinth and Loutraki brushed a faint wash of colour into the lower reaches of the sky. Elaine and Jessica were sitting in darkness at the edge of the terrace as Geraint reached the top of the steps, the light from the stairwell throwing a slab of brightness across the concrete floor.

"Sífnos and Sérifos," Elaine said. "That's what the bloody islands were called."

"Of course," Geraint said, "Sífnos and Sérifos. I told you they were beautiful names."

"Pity they weren't a bit more memorable then," Elaine said. "Where the hell have you been? How long can it take to check your email?"

Geraint could see the whites of her eyes and a flash of teeth as she spoke. "I walked round town for a while," he said. "What's the matter?"

"The matter is, it's ten-thirty," Elaine said.

"It's my fault," Jessica said. "I'm not usually this late."

"Everything's shut," Elaine said. "Can't get hold of any ferry companies, and that damn policeman isn't answering his mobile. If you'd remembered the names of the bloody islands, or if either of you had thought of telling me about this note a bit sooner, we could have been following this up by now, we could have been on to it." Geraint heard her draw in a breath, a sharp, nasal snort of contempt and irritation. "You're busy talking about messages and traces, but the only clue we've actually got, and you neglect to mention it." He started to say something, but she raised her voice, riding over his. "Listen," she said. "You seem to think that something Aled wrote himself, last week, isn't as interesting as an inscription some fucker carved in stone two thousand years ago." In the darkness, Geraint could see her shake her head as a splinter of light from the stairwell caught her ear-rings. "Give me strength," she said.

"He talked about quite a lot of islands," Jessica said softly. "We talked about Kythera, and Santorini, and Ios."

"They're all beautiful names," Geraint said. "And there are hundreds of them."

"But only two he wrote down," Elaine said. "I'm going to bed."

Chapter Thirteen

Kazantsakis met them on the steps of the apartment building. He was in shorts and sandals again.

"We'll go to a place I know," he said, glancing back at the building. "The coffee is better than Mr Panagiotis." He led the way, taking the road to the left along the beach, his sandals clapping softly as he walked. "I didn't have breakfast yet," he said.

The four of them settled themselves at a table, Kazantsakis pulling up chairs for Elaine and Angela with elaborate courtesy, ordering food. "May I see the note you told me?" he said. He smoothed the piece of paper out on the table in front of him. "Sífnos, Sérifos, very nice place. *I'm running out of time,*" he read, nodding to himself. "This is interesting." He looked up, his glance flicking between Elaine and Angela. "And he wrote this to Miss Jessica," he said. "Where is she today?"

"He was running out of time because his two weeks were coming to an end," Angela said.

"She gave it to me last night," Elaine said. "I haven't seen her this morning."

"She doesn't work on a Saturday," Geraint said. "She's probably sleeping in."

"I know," Kazantsakis said.

"I was thinking about going to Kenchrea with her," Geraint said. "Maybe later today, to the sunken harbour."

The waiter came to the table with a tray, setting down coffee and pastries. Kazantsakis gestured at the food.

"Please," he said. He looked at Geraint, raising his eyebrows. "I know the sunken harbour, of course. Very interesting place."

Geraint cleared his throat, aware of the three of them looking at him.

"We need to follow this up right now," Elaine said. "Where are these islands, where do you get a ferry from?"

"Piraeus," Kazantsakis said. "Nearly everything go from Piraeus."

"So somebody needs to get down there, check the ferry companies, see if he got on a boat."

"Can't you just send someone?" Angela said. "Or get the police there to look?" Kazantsakis cut a slice of pastry and sipped his coffee.

"At Piraeus it's not so easy," he said. "They don't keep lists, they don't take ID, you buy a ticket, get on the boat."

"That's ridiculous," Angela said. The policeman shrugged.

"It's what they do," he said. "It's like a railway station, not an aeroplane." He held up his hand as Angela opened her mouth to speak. "But we send somebody to Piraeus, of course. We ask in the shipping offices, talk to people, put up the posters. Maybe something happen, somebody remember; of course." He ate a piece of pastry, watching them. "And I will talk to my colleagues in Sérifos and Sífnos of course, make sure they have the fax, put posters, make some enquiries."

"I think we should go there ourselves," Angela said. "To the islands." Kazantsakis shrugged.

"Take five, maybe six hour," he said.

"Jessica said he talked about lots of islands," Geraint said. "There are hundreds. Where are you going to begin?"

"With the ones he wrote in the note," Angela said. "The note to precious bloody Jessica."

Kazantsakis ate another piece of pastry.

"My advice," he said. "We make enquiries first here, at Piraeus, email some people on the islands. Mr Powell is right, there is a lot of islands."

"It's better than just sitting here," Angela said.

Kazantsakis clicked his fingers for the waiter. He paid the bill, and the two men exchanged a series of rapid phrases, shaking hands. The detective got to his feet.

"Please enjoy the cake," he said. "I will go to Mr Panagiotis apartment building, I would like to talk to Miss Jessica. Then I send a man to Piraeus. May I take the note with me?" Elaine nodded. "We can make some progress now," he said.

"I hope he arrests her," Angela said, watching the policeman thread his way between the tables to the street.

"He may be right," Elaine said. "It might be better to make enquiries on the mainland before we rush off to the islands. We could go to Piraeus, take some posters with us."

Geraint looked at his watch.

"About two hours to Athens by bus," he said. "I think they go about every hour. Then a metro to Piraeus."

"I think I want to do that," Elaine said. "Maybe I'll get Aristotle Enquiries to send someone as well. With the police there, and us, and a private detective, if there's anything to find, we ought to maximise our chances."

"I suppose I better change my clothes," Angela said. "Why am I so tired all the time?" She got to her feet. "I'll see you back at the apartment," she said. Elaine nodded, looking down at her own clothes. She was wearing a linen suit, cream-coloured and elegantly crumpled.

"I think I'll do," she said. "I think I'm OK."

Geraint looked at her, smiling.

"I think you are," he said. He finished his coffee.

"I don't think I'll come to Piraeus," he said. "I want to go to Kenchrea." She looked up at him quickly. "There's enough of you," he said. "What am I going to add? We might as well divide our forces."

"If you think so," she said.

"This place, the sunken harbour, made a big impression on him," Geraint said. "I want to try and find out why. Also, Jessica talks to me. She seems to trust me. I really think she's our best hope of finding out what's happened, and it's hard to do when Angela's around."

Elaine shrugged.

"Might be true," she said. "I suppose it can't do any harm. And you're right, you won't add much at Piraeus."

In Corinth it was market day, and the main square by the bus station

141

had become a shanty town of wood and canvas stalls. Geraint and Jessica pushed slowly through the crowds, passing stalls of melons, the waxy sheen of aubergines, tiny iridescent fish in trays of crushed ice.

"Did Kazantsakis give you back the note?" Geraint asked. Jessica nodded.

"It's the only thing of his I have," she said with a quick smile. "We need a 192, direction Examília and Loutró Eléni."

"I wouldn't want to see it end up in a police file," Geraint said. The southern fringes of Corinth dragged themselves out through suburbs, a cloud of yellow dust following the bus. "How long have you been here?" Geraint asked. "Teaching here?"

"Nearly a year," Jessica said. She leaned her head against the warm, vibrating glass of the window, watching a boy on a scooter overtaking them. "God it's gone fast."

"Do you think you'll stay?"

"Depends," she said. "I haven't really planned that far ahead. I like it here, and there isn't much to go home for." She looked at him with a smile. "Sounds a bit depressive, doesn't it? What I mean is, my parents got divorced last year, my sister's left home, I couldn't find a job I fancied after Uni." She laughed. "It's sounding worse and worse, what a sad life."

The bus conductor nodded at them and pressed the bell.

"Kenchrea," he said, "stop here."

The road had been running in the lee of a steep slope of scrub and stunted trees, the sea on their left. A dirt track led them down between newly built houses to a pebbled bay. They walked across the shingle. Jessica picked up a flat stone and flicked it out across the water, watching it skip over the surface.

"Did you and Aled talk about the future?" Geraint asked. "Maybe that's a stupid question."

"Not really," she said. "I suppose it hung there." She glanced at him. "We didn't have a lot of time together."

"No," he said. He threw a pebble into the water, watching it disappear without a skip, without a splash.

"It's that way," Jessica said, pointing to a couple of small buildings set back from the beach a hundred metres away. Geraint squinted in the bright light, making out low walls running down the beach and into the sea. Around them, the water was disturbed, chopping into little waves.

"This was a massive harbour once," he said. "I've been reading about it." He pointed across the bay to their left. "There was a huge sea-wall from that headland to halfway across the bay. There were sanctuaries of Poseidon and Aphrodite here, and Isis, and Asklepios." Inland from the shingle, the site was half overgrown with wiry scrub and thorns, empty, melancholy in the heat and loud with cicadas. A row of marble column bases led down towards larger structures at the water's edge. "What did Kazantsakis want to talk about?" Geraint asked, watching Jessica as she stepped up on to a block of dressed stone. "This morning, when he gave you back the note?"

A lizard flickered across the face of the stone and into the underbrush.

"He wanted to talk about Angela," Jessica said. "He wanted to know what Aled had said about her, to me." Taking long strides, she stepped from block to block, following the line of the colonnade. Geraint followed her. She stopped and turned to face him, shading her eyes against the sun. "There was nothing to tell him," she said. "Aled never said anything about her. He never mentioned her to me. It was a bit of a shock, meeting her." Geraint nodded. "She's very beautiful."

"It was a bit of a shock for her too," Geraint said. "Meeting you."

At the water's edge the air was cool and salty. They followed the stone pier out until it dipped below the surface. The harbour was like a stone ship, low in the water, pushing out into the bay.

"St Paul sailed from here," Geraint said. "When he left Corinth. He got a ship here and sailed to Ephesus." He gestured to the east. "Over there, in Turkey, sailing past Aigina and Kythnos, and Ikaria." Where Icarus is buried, he thought; his father recovered his body from the sea and buried him on the island. The wings were just a shower of feathers, blown anywhere.

Around them, below the surface, in waves of light, there might be granaries and store houses, doorways, and silent terraces. Geraint

143

thought of the drowned villages of Wales, the church towers under the lake, fish swimming through blind windows.

"She doesn't like me very much, anyway," Jessica said. She crouched at the edge of the pier, staring down into the water, trying to see through the dancing glitter of the surface. "You were asking why he liked this place? He said it was like the moment you take a decision." She looked up at him. "It's the way it hangs here between the land and the sea. It's the boundary between before and after."

"That's exactly right," Geraint said with a sudden excitement. "It's a threshhold. It's the liminal point, the moment everything changes, the first step of the pilgrimage." He looked out across the bay, through the gap between the sheltering headlands, to where the open sea was running. "St Paul shaved his head just before he left here," he said.

Jessica looked at him, squinting in the sunlight.

"No kidding," she said.

"It's a ritual of transition," Geraint said, laughing. "Seriously, it marks the beginning of the journey, the point of no return. The traveller knows he won't come back, that he can't come back, not as the same person."

St Brygga would have performed some equivalent rite, he thought, after the white hound summoned her. The symbolism of leaving was easy to miss at a modern port like Corinth, with its yachts and powerboat moorings. It was precisely here, on the contrary, here where they were standing, that the liminal could be sensed so clearly.

"Life-changing events have three stages," Geraint said. "Do you know about this?" For a moment he could see Janice, tracing arabesques in the twilight with her cigarette as she elaborated the point. "In rites of passage, that kind of thing, you get separation, liminality, return." He numbered them off on his fingers. "The pilgrim has to separate himself, he has to be alone, he has to break away from normal life. That's the first stage." He leaned down and trailed his hand in the water. In the shallows, a fallen column lay half buried in the shingle; black basalt, as dark and perfect as the barrel of a gun. "Then there's liminality," he said. "The threshhold, the door into another world, where the rules of life are inverted, the domain of the spiritual. Life is turned upside down, like a reflection in water. You have to ask yourself:

which is the right way up?" He watched the little waves break and swirl, disrupted, as they crossed the unseen structures of the harbour below them. He glanced across at her. "Finally there's return," he said. "You come back as a different person, transformed."

"So you do come back then," Jessica said.

There was no one at the ticket booth, but the door to the little Museum stood half-open. It was one room, not much more than a stone hut, stifling and dusty. Dying flies vibrated in tiny bursts of energy against the window. There was a section of fluted column, some flagstones leaned against the wall, a fragment of ornate carving from a Corinthian capital. Facing them as they came in was the lower half of a broken statue, long bony toes in Roman sandals. One wall was taken up with an artist's impression of how the harbour would have looked in classical times. There were postcards and leaflets for sale on the counter, and a visitors' book with a pen on a piece of string. Geraint turned back a page, stooping over the book. *A good place to make a decision*, Aled had written. *This is where I make up my mind to go forward not back.*

Jessica swayed against him for a moment as she read over his shoulder.

"I never saw him write this," she said. "I didn't know he'd written this."

★ ★ ★

"This is what he wrote," Geraint said. He passed the piece of paper to Elaine. "I photographed it as well." Angela pulled her chair closer to Elaine's, leaning over to read the note.

"This doesn't look like his handwriting," she said.

"I copied it out, Angela," Geraint said. "I couldn't very well take the visitors' book away."

"I don't see why not," Angela said.

"We've had a really hard day," Elaine said, intercepting his look. "You have no idea how hot it was at Piraeus. Give us a break please, Geraint." She read the note again, shaking her head and leaning back in her chair. The two women were flushed and stunned with heat; it radiated off them in pulses that seemed compressed into a kind of steam by hours of walking in crowded streets, through gritty, exhausted air and the uproar of traffic.

"I'll get you a cold drink," Jessica said, getting to her feet.

"Just water," Angela said, her eyes following the other girl as she crossed the terrace. "How can you be sure it was his handwriting?" she asked Geraint. He shrugged.

"When you know, you know," he said. "There isn't any doubt about it."

"Do you think she takes drugs?" Angela said, her eyes flicking across the terrace in the direction of the stairs. "Do you think that's what this is all about?"

She took the note from Elaine. "*Forward not back,*" she said, her voice rising. "What's that supposed to mean?" Jessica came back with a tray and set out bottles of beer and mineral water. "None of this sounds like Aled," Angela said, looking at her. "It's like he's been drugged."

"It doesn't sound like that to me," Jessica said.

"Perhaps that's only to be expected," Angela said.

Geraint poured a beer and passed it to Elaine. Angela shook her head, reaching for a bottle of water.

"If you're accusing me of taking drugs, I don't," Jessica said.

"She's not accusing you," Geraint said. "Are you?" Angela glared at him.

"What I'm saying, this is not normal," she said. "Anyway, it was you going on about your saints and your stones and your bloody pilgrims that started all this. He never would have come here but for you. None of this would have happened. He never thought about that kind of stuff before you started going on."

"Going on?" Geraint said. "I think it's called being brought up by an archaeologist."

"You didn't actually see him write in the book?" Elaine asked Jessica. The girl shook her head.

"So how do we know he did, then?" Angela said.

"I don't mean that," Elaine said. "I'm looking for some context. When you were at the harbour with Aled, what sort of things were you talking about?"

146

"I think we were talking about making choices," Jessica said. "Deciding what you do with your life, what you want from it. It felt like we were both at one of those moments when you have to choose, when you go one way, or you go another."

"It's a strange place," Geraint said. "It has that kind of effect on you. It's like a doorway, I really felt that."

"So can we expect you to disappear too, then?" Elaine said. Geraint smiled.

"Look," he said. "Is it just me? Don't you feel better for having seen this? Don't you think that, however hard it is for us to understand, Aled is out there somewhere, making choices and decisions for himself?" Jessica nodded.

"That's what I think," she said.

"What would you know?" Angela said. "And who asked you anyway?"

"No need to be like that," Geraint said. Angela drank some water, the glass clicking against her teeth.

"What I'm trying to say, it doesn't make sense," she said. She turned to Jessica. "You might think you know him, but you don't," she said. "He'd never go off like that, with no explanation. Nobody would, but specially not him."

"They do, though," Geraint said. "Unfortunately, they do."

"He's not *they,*" Angela said.

"But he has," Jessica said.

"I think you're missing something here," Elaine said. She leaned forward in her chair. "Finding this note doesn't make everything alright." She looked at Geraint. "I think I agree with you, it feels less like we're dealing with a crime, seeing this. But something very strange and scary is going on, all the same. It's all wrong."

"That's exactly what I mean," Angela said. "Thank you." She turned to Geraint. "I shouldn't get so cross," she said. "But you're so busy thinking about where he's gone, or why he's gone, it's like you're missing the main thing, that he has gone. He's just gone, and no one knows where he is."

"He may be in trouble, or danger," Elaine said. "He may not know where he is himself. Maybe nothing criminal is going on, but this isn't normal, it isn't like him. It's like he's had a breakdown. Maybe he has."

"Exactly," Angela said. "Or drugs. What about that Grey Goose man? Maybe he drugged Aled." She picked up the piece of paper again. "Anyway, I think you're just making assumptions. *Forward not back* – that could mean anything. He might be talking about life back home, about his plans for the future." She glanced at Jessica. "It might not have anything to do with being here, all these theories about wanting to find himself, go off and be a hippy or something."

Geraint sighed.

"I'm not suggesting we stop looking for him," he said, "obviously. And we'll have to let Kazantsakis know about the visitors' book." He turned to Elaine.

"Anyway, what happened at Piraeus? How did you get on?"

"Hopeless," Elaine said. "Impossible."

"You have no idea how hot it was," Angela said. "And it was so noisy, and so much traffic. And its huge, it goes on for ever, it goes on for miles. It was horrible. It's been a horrible day."

"It was pointless," Elaine said. "It was like going down to Southampton and, *asking around*." She framed the last two words in digit finger quote-marks.

"I'm off," Jessica said. "I'm really tired. I'll see you tomorrow."

The twilight had deepened while they'd been talking, falling like a bloom, brushing out the mountains behind the town. Music drifted up to them from the tavernas on the waterfront, and the buzz and grumble of motorbikes. Across the western sky an aeroplane drew a thin line of gold. The lighthouse blinked, turned away.

"See you tomorrow," Angela said, listening to the soft tapping of Jessica's footsteps on the concrete stair. "See you tomorrow, see you tomorrow. Why exactly? Why do we have to see you tomorrow?" She turned to Elaine. "Can't we just tell her we don't need her tomorrow? I really can't stand having her around all the time."

"Don't need her tomorrow?" Geraint said. "She's not a servant, Angela. She's involved, she's got feelings."

"And I haven't?" Angela said. "I'm just supposed to put up with it?"

"This is difficult for everybody," Elaine said.

"And it's thanks to her we've made any progress," Geraint said.

"Right," Angela said. "We mustn't forget all the progress we've made. Like we know where Aled is, like we know he's alright."

"We can begin to imagine he's alright," Geraint said. He reached for the note and folded it into his wallet.

"That's alright then," Angela said bitterly. "We can imagine he's alright. Why don't we imagine he's sitting here, sitting at the table with us. *Hello Aled, how are you? Where did you spring from? Have you had a nice day?*" She got up, pushing her chair back with a short screech of metal on concrete. "I'm going to bed," she said. "I'll leave you to it. I'll leave you to your imagination."

They listened to the clatter of her heels on the steps. Geraint opened a beer; the cap rolled across the table and dropped to the floor, where it spun for a moment, performing a tiny drum-roll.

"That was a bit tiring," he said. "Are you alright? It can't have been much fun in Piraeus." Elaine turned to look out across the bay, her silhouetted profile difficult to interpret. "Jessica's a nice girl," Geraint said. "And she really cares about him. She obviously wants to be involved." He thought about Aled's note, his invitation to Sífnos and Sérifos. "Anyway, she is involved."

"You have to try to be sympathetic to Angela," Elaine said. "She wasn't expecting any of this. It isn't her fault."

"And she really might have more insight into what's happened," Geraint said. "Jessica," he added after a moment. "Not Angela."

"No, not Angela," Elaine said. She lowered her voice. "I shouldn't say that," she said. "I'm not being fair. Nobody's at their best right now."

"Don't forget it must have been just as big a shock for Jessica," Geraint said, "getting confronted with Angela out of the blue."

"Angela, out of the blue," Elaine said. "There's a thought. She certainly is striking, is that the word I'm looking for?"

"Stunning," Geraint said. In the darkness, he could sense Elaine's invisible smile.

"We need to speak to Kazantsakis in the morning," she said into the silence. "And I'd like to go to this internet café, he seems to have mentioned it in every email." Geraint nodded. "Let's not do separate things tomorrow," she said. "Let's look for him together."

Chapter Fourteen

For much of the day, Geraint had the unsettling sense that something had altered in the passage of time; he was aware of discrete episodes, separated by periods of of non-time. Perhaps it was the intensity of the last few days, he thought, which had fused inner and outer states of being. Consciousness articulated itself at one moment as introspective episodes of anxiety or revelation, and at the next by aspects of the outside world: by blinding light, by the scent of resin.

Kazantsakis had been at home when he answered his mobile; Geraint could hear a television, and children's voices. He heard him leave the room or shut a door, his voice suddenly suspended in a featureless background.

"It's like you had a hunch," the detective said. "Like you knew you were going to find something there. That's a strange thing, like you had a message."

"It was things that Jessica talked about," Geraint said.

"Your son and the Jessica," Kazantsakis said. "Maybe that's a problem, with Miss Angela. Maybe I think so."

"Maybe," Geraint said. "Did anything turn up at Piraeus?"

"Not so much," Kazantsakis said. "Sometime people remember something couple of days later. You ask a question they say no, and then next day, *Hey, now I remember something.* Sometimes it goes like that."

The internet place didn't open until midday on a Sunday. They found a table at the back of a dim, old-fashioned café nearby, old men in dark suits reading newspapers, a big three-bladed fan on the ceiling turning slowly.

"I woke up in the middle of the night," Angela said. "I don't know

whether I'd been dreaming or just, you know, thinking in my sleep."
She leaned across the table towards them. "And I had this thought in
my mind: maybe Jessica knows where he is, knows exactly where he
is. Maybe this is all lies, she's just pretending."

Geraint and Elaine glanced at each other.

"But that would be even worse," Geraint said. "Wouldn't it?"

"I wouldn't put anything past her," Angela said. Geraint shook
his head.

"I mean, you find it hard to believe he'd go off without telling
you where he'd gone. But this would be much crueller, wouldn't it?
If he told Jessica and didn't tell us, didn't tell you?" Angela shrugged,
round-shouldered.

"You're right," she said. "I'm not thinking straight."

"Anyway, I believe her," Geraint said. "She's telling the truth, I
know she is. She's doing her best to help."

"That's right," Angela said. "Spring to her defense, Little Miss
Perfect, Princess bloody Pushy. Who does she think she is? She's
certainly got you where she wants you." She sighed, sipped at her
coffee. "Sorry, alright? Anyway, small mercies, at least she's not here
now." She smiled across the table at them. "It's much nicer just the
three of us."

The boy in charge of *Korintho-net* shook Geraint's hand, giving a
little bow to Elaine, rolling his eyes admiringly at Angela.

"I don't see him for a week," he said. "*I pátia gríza,* your grey
duck."

"Does he live here?" Geraint asked. "Is he staying somewhere here?
Do you know what his real name is?"

"He don't live here," the boy said. "Maybe in a hotel, I don't
know." He rubbed his chin, frowning. "Don't know his name," he
said, "just the Duck."

"So, he was sort of a friend of Aled's?" The boy took a step
back, raising his hands in a gesture of pantomime horror, shaking his
head.

"No, not a friend," he said. "Aled and Jessica have a joke, like he's
a CIA, you know? They let him buy a beer, but it's a joke."

"Aled and Jessica," Angela said. "Aled and Jessica. Like on a bloody windscreen. That's the joke. The joke's on me."

The boy glanced at Geraint, lowering his voice. "We have a problem with him," he said. "He like men, you understand? He don't bother Aled," he added quickly. He glanced around the room. There were a couple of teenagers hunched over a terminal at the far end, heads close together, oblivious. "He drink a lot, then he come in here, it's a problem. Last week, at night, the owner talk to him, take him out on the street." The boy smacked his fist hard into the palm of his hand, a short, low punch. "We don't see him after that."

The Tourist Office was about to close for the afternoon. The girl spread a sheaf of brochures and leaflets out on the counter, fanning them open with a practised flourish.

"This is all I have on Ancient Corinth," she said. "I don't hear of this Sanctuary before. Tell me again?"

"Necessity and Violence," Geraint said. "The Sanctuary of Necessity and Violence."

"I never hear of it," the girl said. "Maybe you should try the Museum."

Behind him, Geraint heard Angela let out her breath in a groan. "Or email here," the girl said. She opened one of the brochures and pointed out an address, tapping the page with a lacquered fingernail. "Here, the Department of Antiquities." She gathered the brochures together and handed them to Geraint.

"Have a nice day," she said.

"Aled and I talked about it," Geraint said to Elaine. "It's such a strange name, don't you think?" They crossed the road to the shaded side of the street. "I asked him to try and find it while he was here."

"And did he?" Elaine asked.

"I don't know," Geraint said. "He mentioned it a couple of times in his emails. I should have asked in the Museum when we were there, but I forgot all about it when we found the Briggana inscription. I asked Jessica, but she didn't seem to know anything about it."

"So she doesn't know everything then," Angela said. "That's reassuring."

"The sunken harbour got us the note in the visitors' book," Geraint said. "The Sanctuary could be the same; it has to be worth following up. I think we should go to Ancient Corinth, see if we can find someone at the Museum." Elaine shrugged, nodded. Geraint looked at Angela. "Unless you've got a better idea," he said.

The Museum was closed, the building locked and shuttered behind its melancholy screen of cypresses.

"Pity the girl in the Tourist Office didn't think to tell us," Elaine said. "Save us the bloody bus journey."

Geraint looked up at the Citadel, massed like a thundercloud above the ruined city, the ragged line of fortifications just visible at the summit.

"The damn Sanctuary could be anywhere," he said.

"This never happens to Indiana Jones," Angela said.

There weren't any taxis about, and they had to wait an hour for a bus back to Corinth.

"Indiana Jones and the Temple of Necessity," Elaine said, scuffing at the dusty ground with the toe of her shoe. "Sounds like a public toilet."

★ ★ ★

He'd forgotten to set the alarm, and his phone woke him on Monday morning, the ringing tone distorted and indecipherable, the soundtrack to a dream that vanished the moment he opened his eyes.

"I have some big piece of news," Kazantsakis told him. "Can you hear me?" Geraint mumbled into the phone, propping himself up on one elbow. "Your son's credit card," the policeman said. "It's used in Athens on Saturday morning. It takes out five hundred euros from a bancomat on Adhrianoú Street, centre of city." Geraint cleared his throat, sitting up in the bed and dragging a hand through his hair. "Bancomat of *Ethníki Trápeza,* National Bank," Kazantsakis said. "On Adhrianoú, centre of town, at eleven o'clock. I give you the name and phone number of my colleague, you have a pen?"

"The police station is on Othónos Street, just off Syndágma Square," Geraint said. "We're to ask for Detective Nikodhímos; he'll be expecting us."

He spread the Athens street plan out on the table, Elaine and Angela crowding round him to look over his shoulder. "Here's Syndágma

154

Square. And here's Adhrianoú, where the ATM is." The three of them stared at the map in silence for a moment. "It's a hell of a long street," Geraint said, tracing its angular progress with the tip of his finger.

Angela reached over and pointed at the map.

"So he was right here," she said. "On Saturday morning. While you were swanning around in your precious harbour."

"There was no way to know that," Geraint said.

"The visitors' book doesn't look quite so useful now," Angela said.

"It would make sense to take overnight bags," Elaine said.

"I better tell Jessica what's happening," Geraint said.

The bus was nearly full. Geraint sat across the aisle from Elaine and Angela, cramped in his seat by the bulk of the woman sitting next to him.

Jessica had stared at him, standing in the doorway of her room in her nightdress, her eyes full of sleep.

"This feels awful," she said. "This feels worse than not knowing anything."

"We'll go straight to the police station," Geraint said. "Maybe they have more information by now."

"It's so horrible, all this business with the police," Jessica said. "It's so public, and impersonal." She bit her lip. "I so want to come with you, but I just can't miss my class tonight. They've got exams this week." She shook her head, her lips pinched.

"There's no need for you to come," Geraint said. "I'll text you if there's anything new. Anyway, what if he turned up here and we were all gone?"

"You promise to tell me as soon as you know anything? As soon as you get there?"

"Of course," he said.

"Athens is so big," Jessica said.

The bus had cleared the fringes of the town and was running along the open highway, the sea running with them on their left, the air-conditioning a soft roar over their heads. Twisting round in his seat, Geraint watched as the face of the citadel filled the rear windows of the bus, darkening the sky until it dipped away and was lost in a curve of the road. The cleft of the Canal under their wheels was a blink of

155

discontinuity, felt rather than seen.

Elaine reached over and tapped his arm, and he leaned out into the aisle to catch what she was saying.

"We don't know what we're looking at here," she said. "Credit cards get lost, or stolen."

"I know," Geraint said. "I wonder if there's any way to tell who's using it."

The motorway was running below marble cliffs, through tunnels, on elevated sections cantilevered out over the sea; on the horizon the hazy peaks of the Peloponnese ranged away towards Epidaurus. They passed Eleusis again, the tankers' graveyard in the Bay of Salamis. He called out to Angela.

"Do you remember Eleusis," he said, pointing out the window. "It's only a week since we were here, it doesn't seem possible." Angela glanced out of the window, closed her eyes again.

"It's been completely different from what I thought it would be," Angela was saying to Elaine. "We've spent most of our time worrying about that girl." She leaned back in her seat with a sigh. "But now it's better, going to Athens, this is how it's supposed to be. Now it's like we're a family."

Gradually, in an order reversed from their journey a week before, the landscape revealed its progressive tranformations: semi-developed tracts of light industry and warehousing, the flow of traffic clotting and slowing as the road was joined by tributaries feeding in from disordered jungles of industrial shanty-town, shimmering under a visible layer of pollution in the western approaches to Athens.

"Yes," Elaine was saying into her phone. "No." She pinched the bridge of her nose in a gesture that was eerily familiar. "No," she said again. "I haven't got the files with me. I'm on a bus, on the way to Athens. Call Sharon, get her to email you. Tell her I said it was OK for you to have them." She shut the phone.

"Closed circuit TV," Geraint said. "If there were cameras in the street, maybe they filmed the person who used the card."

"The person who used the card," Angela said. "If the card's been stolen, where does that leave your theory that he's gone off to find himself?"

156

"I'm trying to keep an open mind," Geraint said. "This morning you were accusing me of wasting time at Kenchria while Aled was in Athens. We don't know what's going on, that's the point."

"Where the hell is Kenchria?" Angela asked him

"Let's see the police first," Elaine said. "Let's take it from there."

"The harbour," Geraint said, "the sunken bloody harbour."

The road had been climbing for some time, the bus stopping and starting in the heavy traffic. Now, as they crested the ridge, the city revealed itself below them, filling the bottom of a shallow bowl of landscape as though it had been poured there, flowing across the plain in every direction until it ran up and broke against the feet of distant mountains circling the horizon. Geraint saw Elaine murmur something to herself, shaking her head. The three of them stared out of the bus windows in silence. Far in the middle distance Geraint thought he saw the Acropolis for a moment, sailing like a ship above the city, and a tiny golden shape that must have been the Parthenon. Then the bus was over the rim of the bowl and slipping downhill into the bifurcating canyons of the city's streets, taller buildings blocking the vistas and throwing down valleys of shadow.

From the bus station they took the metro to Syndágma Square. In the corridors of the underground they passed a dozen Missing posters, mostly children, a couple of young men, one of them British, not Aled.

"I heard in Great Britain you have a lot of cameras on the street," Detective Nikodhímos said. He was middle-aged, thin, nervy, very dark. When he took his sunglasses off, he looked incomplete. "But here in Greece it's not so many." He shrugged. "We put his picture at the bancomat now today. If he sees it, I think he calls in, maybe, if he use the bancomat again. Or someone see him."

Geraint put his finger on the little circle the detective had drawn on his street plan, marking the location of the bank.

"Next left should be Adhrianoú Street," he said.

"Won't the bank stop the card?" Angela said.

"Not if he told them he was going to Greece," Elaine said.

"We wouldn't want them to," Geraint said. "While the card's being used we can follow it, maybe catch up."

157

"If it's been stolen it's going to cost us a lot of money," Angela said.

"I don't think that's the main thing at the moment," Geraint said. He was aware that the card was acting as an obstacle to his imagination, to his ability to picture his son as he'd pictured him at Ancient Corinth or the sunken harbour. As Jessica had said, somehow it seemed worse than knowing nothing at all.

Adhrianoú was lined on both sides with gift shops, all displaying the same iconic motifs: owls, goddesses, temples, athletes. A mass of shoppers and sightseers, filling the street from side to side, promenaded vacantly from shop to shop. In Corinth we were parallel to this world, Geraint thought, to this world of tourism and representation, where everything is symbolic, intentional, artificial, ambiguous. The other world, in Corinth and Liminidhi, is formed by self-contained and stable sets of relationships: between past and present, work and rest, light and dark. How will we ever find him in this chaotic world?

"There it is," Angela said, pointing through the crowds.

The bank was on a corner, the ATM recessed into the wall to the left of the glass front doors. Aled's picture had been put up on the inside of the glass. If you were using the cash point and glanced to your right, you would see it.

"It's shut," Angela said, trying the brass door handle.

"What could they have told us?" Elaine said. Her phone was ringing. "No, those are the wrong ones. Ask Sharon for the Lancaster Gate file. Just get her to email everything to you." The cash machine's display was almost opaque in the glaring sunlight. Shading it with his hands, Geraint could just make out a short column of national flags and alternative languages. A passer-by bumped him from behind, a man's voice murmuring *Entschuldigung*. "If she sends you everything, then you can pick out what you need," Elaine said. "I have to go." She stepped off the pavement to let a Japanese couple pass.

The buttons of the keypad were worn smooth and shiny with use. Geraint tried to picture Aled stooped over the machine, just here, two days ago. He tried to picture his hands, an index finger jabbing at the keys. He couldn't form the image. He straightened up. A man gestured at him, smiling, wanting to use the machine.

"This is impossible," Angela said. She stumbled, tripping on the kerb as she was pushed and jostled.

"We ought to stick around here for a while, surely?" Geraint said. Angela looked at him.

"In case he just comes strolling by?" she said.

"Yes," Geraint said, "exactly."

"At least he won't have Jessica on his arm, that's something," Angela said. She backed herself up to the wall, her face working in distaste and irritation as a group of teenagers pressed past them.

"We need somewhere to stay tonight," Elaine said. "We mustn't leave it too late to find somewhere half-decent."

"But not yet," Geraint said, glancing at his watch. "There's plenty of time yet."

"What exactly is the plan?" Angela said. "How long are we going to stay here? A day, two days, a week? And are we going to stay right here?" she said. "By the cash point?"

"I don't know," Geraint said.

"If he was in Athens on Saturday, he may still be here," Elaine said, watching the crowds passing. "I know it seems hopeless, but what else can we do?"

"They only put the poster up today," Geraint said. "If he sees it he may get in touch. He may not know we're here, looking for him."

"Good point," Angela said. "He probably thinks it's quite normal to just disappear without telling anyone."

"We don't even know it was Aled who used the card," Geraint said. "This is just the best of a bad set of choices."

"Don't you want to look at some temples?" Angela said. "There must be plenty of temples here. Perhaps you'll find another fascinating inscription, or a statue or something. Maybe you'll find a statue that looks exactly like him."

"Let's find somewhere to have a drink," Elaine said. "Somewhere we can watch the street from."

"There's another word that anthropologists use," Geraint said. "*Communitas*. It's connected with the liminal thing." Elaine sighed. "It means the mystical bonds of love and community that form between people in a group of pilgrims. Their lives and their relationships are changed forever." He raised the tall, icy glass of pale blonde beer in a toast. "On that note, cheers Angela," he said.

"We could take it in turns to stay here all night," Angela said. "Watching the ATM."

Eventually, they found a small hotel on Thisseos Street, the other side of Syndágma Square from the police station.

"I never thought everywhere would be so full," Elaine said. "We were lucky to find this dump."

There was no air-conditioning, and the room was stifling. The window opened onto a narrow well of grey walls and washing lines; the outside air was damp and stale, smelling of steam. Geraint walked out into the corridor and tapped on Elaine's door.

"I'm going for a walk," he said. "Are we going to meet up later, find somewhere to eat?"

"Maybe not," she said. "Everywhere is going to be so busy and full, and it's too damn hot."

He heard Angela call out through the thin walls of the next room.

"Definitely not," she said.

Geraint turned left out of the hotel, glancing back to memorise the look of the street, and set off with no destination in mind. He found himself crossing a park, a maze of winding paths under towering colonnades of palm trees. He became aware of the faintly menacing click of worry-beads as someone followed him, walking a little too close. When he glanced over his shoulder, the man turned onto a diverging path and disappeared into the darkness.

He crossed a main road. On the central island, by the traffic lights, a pair of Corinthian columns rose with astonishing elegance into the night sky. The busier squares were filled with restaurants. As Geraint passed, waiters stepped out in front of him, waving menus, trying to herd him to a table. On a wide boulevard he passed the entrance to a metro station, a flight of steps descending steeply into the depths. He thought about the world of the Greek myths, its diagrammatic simplicity: gods, mortals, this life, the afterlife, Olympus, the Underworld. These domains were separate, though sometimes interpenetrable, but journeys between them were always perilous, governed by enigmatic prohibitions, irreversible consequences. The door closed forever, the loved one was lost, or turned to stone, transformed into a tree, a bird, a stag, a breath of wind: *Don't look back, don't look now.*

* * *

"We could get breakfast at the café on Adhrianoú, down from the bank," Geraint said. They stepped out into the street. The air glittered as though washed, still touched with coolness. He felt a wave of ambiguous emotion, perhaps hope, rush through him. "We'd be in the right place then."

"The right place?" Angela said.

"That's right."

"As long as they have proper coffee," Angela said. "Not that mud they serve everywhere." They ordered food, and tall glasses of milky coffee. Elaine's phone rang and she got up and walked off a few paces, talking intently. "We can have lunch here too," Angela said. "And supper." Elaine snapped her phone shut and came back to the table. "We can sit here day and night," Angela said.

"I've been thinking about this," Elaine said. "I think we should talk to the Consulate again, and obviously to the police here. Maybe to Kazantsakis as well. We need lists of cheap hotels, internet cafés, maybe bars or clubs where young people go. This is a huge city, we have to not be hypnotised by it, we have to try and narrow it down." Geraint nodded.

"We need to keep an eye on this place as well, though," he said.

"We need to split up," Elaine said. "We need to maximise our resources. The police wait for information to come to them. We have to go and find it for ourselves." She scrolled through her phone's address book. "I have a number for a private investigator here," she said. "I'll ring them too. We need to get down to business."

"So that's clubs and bars and internet cafés," Angela said. "The sort of places he's likely to be. We better not forget ancient monuments too, now he's got this passion for temples and harbours." Geraint looked at her, opening his mouth. She held up her hand. "I'm being a stroppy cow," she said. "I had noticed, you know. I'm not always like this."

161

"It's not helping," Elaine said.

"Why don't you try and see it from my point of view, just once," Angela said. "I didn't start off like this. I thought something terrible had happened to him. I still do. I'm worried sick." She glared at Geraint. "You've done your best to convince me that he's gone off on some sort of hippy trip, dumping me in the process, by the way. And the whole thing with that girl, that fucking Jessica." She put her coffee down, the glass chattering in the saucer. "And you're so nice to her. You can't get enough of her. You obviously think Aled would be much better off with her than with me. Did you never stop to think how I was feeling?"

Geraint's phone was ringing.

"Yes," he said. "We're by the bank. Yes." Elaine and Angela watched him, aware of the sudden tension, straining to hear the faint tinny quacking of the voice on the other end of the line. "Alec Poole?" Geraint said. "It could be, couldn't it?" He gestured hectically at Elaine to get the waiter, pay the bill. "We'll be ten minutes."

"What is it?"

"They're holding someone at the police station," Geraint said. "English, they said. They've got his name as Alec Poole, but that could be the guy on the desk writing it down wrong."

"I can't run in these," Elaine said, trotting to keep up as they dodged out into the crowds.

"My God," Angela said.

"Shouldn't we get off this street and find a cab?" Elaine said.

"Quicker on foot," Geraint said.

Nikodhímos was waiting for them on the steps of the police station.

"Take a minute," he said. "Take your breath back. Come out of the sun." He led them into the lobby of the station. "It's better in here. So, they bring him in this morning." He rubbed his chin, watching them, impassive behind his sunglasses. "He's very dirty," he said, "maybe living in the street, maybe not well in the health. Police doctor is with him now, also later we get psychologic report. When I talk to him he is confused."

He led them down a long corridor into the heart of the building.

162

The clacking of Elaine's heels echoed off the walls, cracking off the ceiling as though they were walking upside down. The police doctor nodded to them as he opened the door for them, patting Nikodhímos on the shoulder.

The boy was no more than sixteen or seventeen, skinny, red-haired. He was holding himself very straight in the chair.

"I'm Alec," he said. "I'm Alec. Have you come for me?"

Geraint heard Elaine let her breath out in a long shuddering sigh. Nikodhímos shook his head, glancing at the doctor, spreading his hands out in a gesture that was resigned, accepting, fatalistic.

"I'm sorry," he said.

"Wait," the boy said. "Wait. I'm Alec. You know me, you must know me."

"Where are you from, darling?" Elaine said. "What's been happening to you?"

"From there," he said, jerking his head in an awkward, sideways movement. "I'm from down there." There was a silence. Geraint and Elaine looked at each other. "I think I want to stop now," the boy said.

"Where do you live, sweetheart?" Elaine said. "Where's your home?"

"Sweetheart," the boy said, smiling at her, his eyes glistening. "Sweetheart."

Nikodhímos saw them to the front steps of the police station, shaking hands with each of them.

"We don't give up," he said.

The freshness of the morning had boiled away as they turned the corner of the street into the steely brightness of Syndágma Square.

"Maybe this whole thing is my fault," Elaine said. Geraint glanced at her. She folded the list of addresses that Nikodhímos had given them, tucking them into her handbag. She handed Geraint the folder of Missing posters. "Can you take this," she said. "I need to sit down. I need a glass of water."

They crossed at the lights, a wall of traffic growling tensely at them, penned up behind the red light.

"How is it your fault?" Geraint asked.

163

"That poor boy," she said. "He was so lost."

The waiter brought a tall bottle of mineral water and glasses, slices of lemon.

"They should think about it," Angela said. "These kids, when they're taking drugs, they should think about what can happen."

"Not everything's drugs," Geraint said.

"I expect you think he was on a journey," Angela said. "Looking for himself. He didn't get very far."

"He was a child," Elaine said. "At that age you're a child." She put her sunglasses on, the reflecting lenses panning across hotels, palm trees, broad flights of steps, as she turned her head. "I thought Aled would be fine," she said, turning to Geraint. "When I moved out he'd finished his exams, all his friends were back there with you." She was turning the glass of water in her hands, watching the bubbles rushing to the surface. "I thought he'd come up lots of weekends, holidays. It would be like having two homes." In front of the Parliament Building the soldiers in their absurd uniforms pranced and stamped and turned, clouds of pigeons rising and scattering in front of them. "How much time has he spent with me in London, in the last five years?" she said. "Hardly any. I guess he never liked Steve much, but I always felt that wouldn't really matter, we'd be together anyway, I would always be his mum, nothing would ever come between us." She looked out into the square, following the surging traffic for a moment, as you watch a stick in the river. "But maybe he thought I'd let him go," she said. "Do you know what I mean? Maybe he thought that I'd let go of him."

"He's never thought that," Geraint said.

"Somebody let go of that boy in there," she said. "That poor Alec, somebody let go of him."

"I don't see how it was your fault," Angela said. "Aled was really happy, everyone knows that. Until he came out here, anyway." She looked at Geraint. "We were happy together, why else do you think we were getting married?"

Elaine drew a deep breath. "Hostels and budget hotels in central Athens," she said "Internet cafés, bars, nightclubs. How are we going to approach this?"

164

They looked at each other. Above the Parliament Building the Greek flag stirred and lifted.

* * *

"*Yiós mou*," Geraint said. "My son. Have you seen him?" His shirt was sticking to his back. From time to time he felt the progress of an individual drop of sweat, rolling from armpit to waistband. "*Ekasa yiós mou.* I've lost my son. Do you speak English? Do you recognise this picture?"

Using his section of the list he worked his way south west from Syndágma in the direction of the Plaka and the Acropolis, across the heat of the main boulevards, into the slots of narrow alleys, through shady squares, down cobbled flights of steps and out again into the traffic. "*Ekasa yiós mou.* I've lost my son."

He located Hotel Achilléas and the Kouros, Hotel Petráki, Central Students Hostel, Athens Bargain Rooms, Hostel Olympos, Sotíros Rooms To Let. He spoke to old men behind desks and young women in reception booths, to students practising their English, to a carpenter fixing a window frame, to groups of back-packers sitting on the steps of open doorways consulting maps. At one of the bigger places he got them to photocopy his last poster. They could only do monochrome, the shades of grey imposing another degree of separation on the image.

He sat in the café on Adhrianoú waiting for Elaine and Angela. The prospect of the evening ahead, checking the bars and clubs on the police list, pressed him down into his chair, like the onset of an illness. He thought about poor Alec Poole, in his own antechamber of the underworld. The doorway he had slipped through on some impulse led down into the dark, and he had lost the thread that might have led him back out into the light. *I come from down there. Have you come to get me?*

A police helicopter passed overhead, a blue light flicking irritably on its underside. As the thud of the aircraft faded away over the Acropolis, Geraint became aware of his phone ringing.

"Janice," he said. "It's so nice to hear your voice. What's wrong with texting though? This is going to cost you."

165

"Actually it's costing you," Janice said. "I'm phoning from your house. I got the key and dropped in like you asked."

"We're in Athens," Geraint said. "The police told us his credit card's been used here." He let his breath out in a short sigh. "This place is huge Janice, it goes on forever. In Corinth you can believe that a person leaves a trail, that there'll be signs that you can follow, but this is a labyrinth, you feel like you've gone blind. I spent all afternoon going round cheap hotels, it's a nightmare."

"I'm so sorry," Janice said. "Listen."

"We just have to keep trying," Geraint said. "I don't see what else we can do."

"Wait," Janice said. "Geraint, listen. There's a letter here for you with a Greek postmark. Do you want me to open it, read it to you?" The waiter gestured at the empty beer glass. Geraint shook his head. "Did you hear me?" Janice asked. "Are you still there?"

"Yes," he said. "Open it. You'd better open it."

Part Three

Return

Chapter Fifteen

It was raining over Cardiff, and windy, the aeroplane dropping down through rags of wet and grey in a series of jolts and side-slips.

"By the way, I phoned Mam from Athens," Angela said. "Dad's going to come and meet me. You won't need to drive me back to Llanfrychan."

"Fine," Geraint said. "Good idea."

Her suitcase was among the first through the rubber flaps of the carousel; she wrenched it off the moving belt and walked away without looking back, the little wheels drumming dully behind her. Around him, waiting for their cases, disconsolate groups of fellow-passengers shuffled and stared. In the car park the rain was combing through the puddles. Geraint joined the line of cars queuing to leave the airport, the barrier rising and falling, his thoughts dulled by the thump of the windscreen wipers.

By the time he got home the light was failing. The house was cold and empty, an absence that was physically evident. Janice had left Aled's letter on the kitchen table, folded back into the envelope. Geraint held it under the hanging lamp, taking in the sloped, impatient handwriting: *Megalo Vretania* – Great Britain. He sat down.

Dear Dad, he read. He ran his fingers over the surface of the paper. This was an object that belonged to a moment, written at a particular point in space. Only the passing of time separated this letter from Aled, so the object itself was precious beyond the words, as love letters are. Janice's transcription in her email to him in Liminidhi had given him information that was abstract in comparison.

Dear Dad, this is going to come as a bit of a shock I think, so I'll start off I'm fine. Geraint read the date at the top of the letter again. *Liminidhi*

168

July 2nd. The day, or the night, before he was booked to fly home, two and a half weeks ago. He tried to read the postmark over the stylised image of the Parthenon on the stamp, but it was blurred and illegible. In any case it had taken over a week to arrive, perhaps more, before landing on the mat in the empty hallway. *It's difficult to explain. If I came back and tried to explain it, I'd be doing the same thing that I've always done, like what other people expect from me. I'd still be on the straight line.*

Geraint leaned back in his chair. Closing his eyes, he could see Adhriánou Street, feel the hot plastic of the phone against his ear. It had taken Janice a long time, over a number of interruptions, to read the letter. She kept stopping, sometimes hesitating over the handwriting, sometimes reading rapidly ahead to herself. They had to wait when the police helicopter came over again. Elaine had arrived, unrecognised for a moment, a woman in a red and white dress glimpsed through the crowd, pushing her hair back with a remembered gesture, never seen without a sudden movement of the heart. Janice had finished by the time Angela arrived. He had quickly improvised an edited version.

"He's says he's writing to you," he had said. "I expect it'll be there when you get back."

He picked up Aled's letter again. *I guess everything about this is odd, when do I write letters, what century are we in? (joke) It's late and I hope this isn't sounding muddled, because in fact I'm not muddled at all.* His phone rang.

"Did you get back alright?" Elaine said. "Are you home yet?" There was a faint click and snap, and he heard her draw a deep breath. "I've started smoking again," she said. "I wanted one so badly on the plane, when they came round with that wretched trolley I thought sod it, I'll have two hundred." She drew in, exhaled. "How was your flight?"

"I'm reading Aled's letter," Geraint said. "I mean, the original. Do you want me to send you a photocopy?"

"Send me the original," Elaine said. "You can copy it." Geraint listened through another long exhalation.

"You're making me want a cigarette," he said.

"Christ, this has been a roller-coaster," Elaine said.

He didn't bother to unpack; he finished reading the letter, read it again, poured himself a couple of drinks, and went to bed. He saw the long piers under the water, the white marble columns, the stone stairs stepping down under the surface. Beyond the sheltering headlands the open sea was running, splashed with white where the waves were cresting.

The rain had cleared overnight, leaving the sky washed and cool, streaked with cirrus. The trees in his mother's road were shivering, and little round-shouldered blackbirds hopped amongst the shrubs in her front garden. Everything was wet and green.

"Another visitor," his mother said, beaming at him. "Where have you been Geraint?"

He followed her into the kitchen. Rosie was sitting at the table, a cup of tea and a plate of biscuits in front of her. They nodded and smiled at each other.

"I've been in Greece," he said. His mother reached down another tea cup from the sideboard.

"Did I know that?" she said. "In Greece?"

"Much have I travelled in the realms of gold," Rosie said. Geraint looked at her. "Where did that come from?" she said, a look of mild astonishment in her eyes.

"It's Keats," Geraint said.

"Is it?" Rosie said. "Keats, is it?"

"Of course I did," his mother said. "You came to see me before you left, just like Rosie did. Aled was there too, wasn't he, or am I getting muddled up? Do you remember, you got the flour down off the top shelf for me. Beti had put it up high, I don't know why she does that."

Geraint shook his head. "No," he said. "No, you're not muddled up."

"I missed most of that rain," Rosie said. "Got back last night. Pretty good up to then, quite warm. I was on that 4371, all the way from Craven Arms to Bourton. That's a good stretch, that."

"When is Aled coming to see me?" his mother asked him. "Why isn't he here?"

"He's still in Greece," Geraint said.

"I went off on by-roads after that," Rosie said. "Hughly, Church Preen. Started to work my way west, back across the A49. Church

Pulverbatch, Snailbeach." She snorted with sudden laughter. "Where do they get those names?"

His mother reappeared from the larder, setting a saucepan on the stove.

"Still in Greece?" she said. "He's been gone a long time, hasn't he? When is he coming back?"

Geraint closed his eyes, finding he could remember Aled's letter almost word for word. "I think he'll be gone for some time," he said.

"Finally picked up the 4386," Rosie said. "That's a B-road of course, through Montgomery, Abermule."

"I remember," Geraint said. "You were looking for windmills. You were up at St Brygga's Chair, I gave you a lift."

"That's right," Rosie said. "So you did. I don't remember any windmills though."

"Do you often go up there?" Geraint asked her. "To St Brygga's Chair?"

"All my journeys start from there," Rosie told him.

"Why is that, do you think?" Geraint asked.

"You've got to start somewhere," Rosie said patiently. "So you might as well start at the beginning."

★ ★ ★

On Monday morning he went into the Museum early, only the cleaners there, banging and singing; he had wanted some time to himself before facing everybody. Sitting down at his desk he was immediately overwhelmed, as he had known he would be, the predator surging through the door, filling the room, engulfing him. He let the feeling wash over him for a while, then leaned forward and switched on his computer.

He heard the postman calling, Gavin whistling as he dragged some heavy object through the front doors. He heard Mike and Nia arrive together, arguing as they clattered up the stairs. A little later Mike appeared in his doorway.

"Good to have you back," he said with his booming, uneasy enthusiasm. "Glad it turned out alright." Geraint watched him as he struggled to find the light touch, the sensitive note that would display his qualities as a manager: caring, insightful, good in a crisis. "Bet you wish he'd taken a gap year now," he said finally.

Geraint was standing at the window, staring down into the rhododendrons when he heard Janice come into the room, knowing it was her before he turned round. She crossed the room and kissed him. He pulled away laughing, but she held onto him.

"Look at me," she said, staring fiercely into his eyes for a moment before letting him go.

"Do you want a coffee?" she said.

Through the afternoon Geraint worked through his emails and letters, discovering from time to time, as his thoughts circled back to the same place, that sadness accumulates simply, like dust, not falling, or arriving from somewhere else, just being there, incrementally, where it wasn't before.

They went to the Bull after work, sitting at a table outside while the pigeons strutted fretfully at their feet.

"You've come back a different person," Janice said. "But then, you knew you would." She looked at him over the top of her pint. "Suntan suits you, I have to say."

"I don't know why it feels so bad," he said. "Somehow he feels further away than when we didn't know anything at all. It's as though he's put himself beyond reach. I suppose that's what he meant to do."

"But you know he's alright," Janice said. Geraint thought about Alec Poole, wondering if anyone had come for him yet.

"I hope he's alright," he said. "That's all I know." From across town, from St Michael's, a bell was tolling. "The trouble with coming back as a different person is that nothing makes sense any more," Geraint said. "It feels like someone drove the Corinth Canal through my life. All those bloody emails this afternoon, that stuff with Mike, it just seems so pointless."

"That's because it is," Janice said. "It really is pointless."

"I'm too tired," Geraint said. "I need to stop thinking about it. If I get you a pint, will you go on with your story?" Janice stood up.

"You're on," she said. "Let's go inside though, it's cold out here, it's like bloody autumn." They settled into deep armchairs on either side of the unlit fire. Geraint leaned back in his chair, closing his eyes. "Where had we got to?" Janice said. "I remember. Your namesake is very tired, my poor fictional Geraint. He's become thinned out, which is why the Grey Goose has power over him. Obsession and melancholia literally wear you out, they rub away your substance until you become transparent, less than a ghost."

"Remind me why he's like this," Geraint said.

"He's lost in reverie and melancholia," Janice said. "Don't you love the sound of those words?" Geraint nodded.

"In a gloomy sort of way," he said.

"Trauma stops time," Janice said. "The afflicted person is trapped in time, endlessly circling the event."

"But what is the event?" Geraint asked.

"The event is his obsession," Janice said. "The moment that the pathogen entered his body, when he first saw the painting: when he first met her. Whatever that virus was, it's consumed him. He doesn't think about going home any more. He has no sense that anyone is missing him, or looking for him, or coming to rescue him."

"How much darker does this get?" Geraint said.

"Wait," Janice said. "See what happens." She lit a cigarette, throwing her head back and breathing out a vertical column of smoke.

"They're standing in front of this massive door in a back street, in an unfamiliar part of the city, it really doesn't look like a restaurant. Do you remember?" Geraint nodded. "The Grey Goose has just said something into the intercom thing, and they're waiting in silence. The American catches Geraint's eye, but it's as though he doesn't see him, he just looks right through him." She glanced round as a couple of men came into the bar, farmers. "The black door starts to open inwards, quite slowly. It must be pitch dark in there, because no light spills out on to the street. Suddenly, to his amazement, Geraint finds that he's running full tilt down the street, back the way they'd come. It's as though the sound of his shoes clattering on the cobbles, echoes flying in every direction, comes to his attention first, followed a moment later by the realisation that he's running as fast as he can, arms and legs scything. His breath is whistling in quick, efficient gasps through his teeth. After what seems like many seconds he hears the heavy thudding of the American's footsteps coming after him. He's in a real sprinter's rhythm now, pumping. When he takes a left at the bottom of the street he's banked over like a motorcycle. He feels like he's flying, he never knew he could run like this. He turns at the next junction onto a bigger street, one or two cars hissing past him. He can't hear the American's footsteps any more, but he doesn't look round to check until the street suddenly opens out and dumps him into the Marienplatz, like emerging out of one of those pipes into a swimming pool." Janice smiled at him. "See?" she said.

"That was pretty good," Geraint said.

"He walks very slowly across the Marienplatz," Janice said. "The lights are bright, there are plenty of people about. He realises that whatever happens next, for the time being he's safe, and best of all he did it himself, he rescued himself. It's a wonderful feeling."

Geraint stared into the ashes of the fireplace. Is that what Aled did, he thought, break loose, get free, rescue himself?

"He's safe too," Janice said, breaking into his thoughts. "You know he is." Geraint shook his head.

"I don't," he said. "I don't know anything. It's like a bomb went off. You think your life is organised, that you know where everything is, where the people that matter to you are, you can find them when you need them. And then suddenly you don't know any of that."

"You haven't lost him," Janice said. "You just don't know where he is. But he does, he knows where he is, better than he did before." There was a silence. "Tell me about your holy woman," she said. "How far did you follow her trail from the inscription?"

"I think I found the exact place she built her oratory," Geraint said. "It's a beach-shop now. You can buy plastic shoes, and inflatable dolphins." They smiled at each other. "They piped her never-failing spring," he said. "It goes under the road and trickles out onto the beach."

"Looking across the bay to the temple on the headland," Janice said. Geraint nodded.

"That's right, I went there. Talking of saints, I saw Rosie on the weekend," he said. "My incarnate holy woman, at my mother's, just

174

back from her travels."

"The mysterious Rosie," Janice said. "An explanation that doesn't explain anything. Anyway, how was she?"

"The same as always."

"Not transformed by the liminal experience?" Janice said. Geraint shook his head.

"Not as far as I could tell," he said. "She seems to pop through the portal and back again without any noticeable transformation. Although she quoted a bit of Keats, come to think of it, that was a surprise."

"That's wonderful," Janice said, her eyes shining. "You see? No one returns unchanged."

"Do they all return though?" Geraint said.

"Of course," Janice said. "I told you. All pilgrims come back." She pulled her chair closer, leaning forward. "Geraint," she said with a kind of urgency, looking intently into his eyes, "don't do it, don't loop."

"Loop?" he said.

"You know what I mean. You're circling, you can't find a straight line, everything brings you back to Aled."

"Yes it does."

"It's dangerous to do that," Janice said. "You can get trapped, it becomes compulsive, it'll wear you out."

"Like my name-sake," Geraint said. "Thanks, Janice."

"He rescued himself, and so can you. He makes a happy future for himself."

"The future's not the problem," Geraint said. "When something terrible happens you know it's going to blight the future. The worst thing is the way it corrupts the past, that's how it really affects you, I never knew that until now. The past becomes nothing more than a state of ignorance, a time when you didn't know what was about to happen."

She looked at him without speaking for a moment.

"He'll come back," she said. "It won't be the same as it was, but you'll see him again. All pilgrims come back."

"Maybe not St Brygga," Geraint said.

"Maybe even her."

* * *

They were working to meet the new deadline for the 1930s school-room on the second floor. The basic carpentry was done, and they were left with text panels and captioning, fitting out. Geraint sat down at a desk, running his fingers over a palimpsest of names carved into the wood: Dafydd Edwards, Beti Protheroe, Gavin Williams. Looking round the room he felt astonished that this work, this place, had persisted unchanged, waiting for him across the gulf of time since he last saw it.

Janice looked in on him half way through the afternoon.

"I was thinking what you said about looping," Geraint said. "About obsessive-compulsive disorder."

"Cheerful subject," Janice said. She tapped ash off her cigarette into the ink-well set into the corner of the desk.

"It's like variations on a theme, in classical music," he said. "You keep returning to the same thing, all the elaborations are just a way of getting back to the same thing."

"There's a set of variations called *La Folia*," Janice said. "Do you know it? I can't remember who it's by, but it means *Madness*: variations on the theme of madness."

"You're always a step ahead," Geraint said, smiling at her.

"Two steps," she said. She walked over to the blackboard on its easel in the corner of the room. "No chalk," she said. "Damn, I was going to write something rude."

He drove round to his mother's after work.

"Where's Rosie?" he asked. "Has she set off again?"

"Rosie?" his mother said.

"Your friend Rosie," he said, "your travelling friend." His mother seemed to come back from somewhere, looking at Geraint with mild surprise.

"Rosie," she said. "She's out walking, she walks every day, says she can't stop. I expect she'll be back soon." She sat down at the kitchen table. "I don't know how she does it. What were you asking me, dear?"

"I'll make us some tea," he said. "You just sit there, I'll do it." His mother smiled at him, her eyes following him as he moved about, finding the caddy, the tea-pot, filling the kettle.

"I want you to explain something to me," she said. "You've probably told me before, but I'm finding it very hard to keep things in my head these days."

Geraint leaned against the sink, waiting for her to go on. "It's Aled," she said finally. "Now, I think you told me he was in Greece, but then the other day you said you were in Greece. Did I get that wrong?"

Geraint shook his head. "No, you're not wrong," he said. "We were both there, at different times." He brought the tea over to the table.

"But if Aled's come back, why hasn't he been to see me?" his mother asked him.

"He hasn't come back," Geraint said. "He's still there."

"You mean you left him there?" she said. Someone clattered the knocker on the front door. "That'll be Rosie," his mother said. "Let her in dear. Where have you been Rosie, where did you go today?"

"Went up to the headland," Rosie said. "Took the 471 out of town, then the Morton lane, then up that track to the top there. Sat on the Saint's chair, looking out to sea." She caught Geraint's eye with a look he couldn't quite interpret: sly, elated. She paused, watching him. "Silent upon a peak in Darien."

"Keats again!" Geraint said, grinning at her. "I meant to bring my copy with me to show you."

"Used to know that poem off by heart," Rosie said.

"Rosie had a very good education," his mother said.

"Forgotten it all," Rosie said. "Most of it."

"Where did you go to school?" Geraint asked.

Behind her, Geraint's mother shook her head, frowning at him.

"A long time ago," Rosie said. "Mind you, sometimes it comes back as if it was yesterday."

"Does it?" Geraint asked, getting another emphatic look from his mother.

"Other times it's like it happened to someone else," Rosie said. "Or never happened at all." She was carrying out little agitated tasks on the table in front of her, folding the newspaper and lining it up with the edge of the table, turning the tea-pot so that its spout faced away from her, moving the sugar bowl. "I should be off," she said.

177

"It's time I was going."

"You're not going today," Geraint's mother said. "You can't go today."

Geraint got to his feet.

"I should be going," he said.

"You've done enough walking for today," his mother said to Rosie. "I'll get dinner started. You stay too, Aled."

"No, I think I'll get going," Geraint said.

"Geraint," his mother said. "Did I just call you Aled? What am I talking about?"

★ ★ ★

He was watching the news when Elaine rang.

"Want to hear something funny?" she said. He heard the snap of her cigarette lighter. "Those bastards."

"What bastards?" Geraint asked. She drew her breath in sharply before answering. "What bastards?" he asked again, smelling the cigarette smoke.

"Those bastards at Aristotle Investigations," she said. "Do you remember? They were going to send someone down to Piraeus."

"I do," he said. "What's happened?"

"They sent in their bill," she said. "They sent me a bill for three thousand seven hundred euros." She gave a short, coughing laugh. "All itemised. They sent two men to the islands, the lunatics, they were there for three days or something, Sifnos and Serifos. Christ almighty, what were they thinking about? Did we ask them to do that? No significant results, needless to say." He heard a faint crunching sound as she stubbed her cigarette out. "I've been keeping in touch with Jessica," she said. "I had an email from her tonight, she hasn't heard from him." So lucidly that he caught the scent of cinnamon, Geraint pictured the main street in Liminidhi, the boy in *Korintho-net* bringing Jessica a tiny cup of sweet grainy coffee as she typed. "I'll talk to Bruce," Elaine was saying. "See what our options are. If we have to pay the bastards, you and I should go halves, obviously."

★ ★ ★

178

He had arranged to meet Lydia on Friday night. The Castle had a function on, so he booked a table at the Stag, recollecting as they walked through the door that they had come here the first night they went out, when he had talked to her about St Brygga. The girl led them to the same table.

"I am so happy for your son," Lydia said. "I lighted a candle for him, I told you, at St Zachariah. They have Greek festival there this month, it's very beautiful."

"Thank you for the candle," Geraint said. Lydia looked at him.

"You were very busy since you came back?" she said.

"Lot of catching up," Geraint said, hearing how flat he sounded. Lydia shrugged.

"Tell me about your visit," she said. "Tell me everything you saw. So beautiful in summer." She glanced at him when he ordered a second bottle of wine, her expression tightening for a moment, but she let him half fill her glass.

"How was it in Athens?" she said. "I miss it so much. Describe it to me."

"I missed him when he went off to college," Geraint said. "But it was limited, and organised, and he was back quite often." He finished the wine in his glass and poured himself another. She shook her head, her hand held elegantly over her glass. "And it was all mixed up with Elaine leaving," he said. "It was difficult to tell one thing from another." She nodded.

"I am sorry for you," she said.

"Athens was terrible," Geraint said, "all those streets. How would you ever find anyone there?"

"It's a big city," she said. "Of course, but so beautiful, don't you find?"

"I feel responsible twice over," Geraint said. "He went there because of me, and I failed to bring him back. Like Orpheus and Eurydice." Lydia looked at him.

"I don't understand," she said.

"Don't look back," he said. "Orpheus looked back to see if Eurydice was following him out of the Underworld, so he lost her forever."

"It's a beautiful story," Lydia said. "Very sad, but it's not like your

179

son."

"I gave him the language," Geraint said. "Maybe he was restless and dissatisfied, but I gave him the words to articulate those feelings, all that stuff about pilgrimage and thresholds and leaving. I put those ideas in his mind." He looked at her, becoming aware that she hadn't understood, or perhaps wasn't listening.

"It isn't death," she said, turning the wine glass by the stem. "It's just loss, Geraint, not death. Your loss, I think." She looked at him. "I think I made my decision. I'm thinking about it for a long time. Maybe the boys don't like it at first, but soon they will be very happy." She raised her glass, pausing for a moment as though suggesting a toast. "Tonight I made my decision," she said. "The boys and I are going back to Greece."

Chapter Sixteen

"Meeting on a weekend," Janice said. "This is exciting." She pulled the door shut, struggling with the seat belt for a moment, arranging herself in the cramped space. Geraint lowered his window, the warm breeze blowing through the car as they drove. She glanced at him when they turned up the Morton lane past Pont Sais.

"Why am I not surprised?" she said.

"Do you mind?" Geraint asked. "Coming back to the beginning?"

Janice shook her head. *"The end of all our exploring will be to arrive where we started,"* she said. *"And know the place for the first time."*

They parked by the plantation and started up the slope towards the headland. The fields on their left had been mown and the drying crop lay in silvery swathes.

"She was quoting Keats again," Geraint said, "when I was at my mother's." The sea opened all around them, shining. They sat down on St Brygga's Chair.

"Is it her?" Janice said. "The older sister, the one who went missing? Has your mother ever said anything?" Geraint shrugged.

"It's getting hard to tell with my poor mother," he said. "She's on a journey of her own. And the way Rosie is, maybe they've never talked about it. Maybe Rosie doesn't know. Perhaps nobody knows." He lay back on the slope of the stone, the sun's blood warm on his eyelids, the sea breathing in long swells at the foot of the cliffs. "You smoke too much, Janice," he said. He felt her lie back on the stone beside him.

"It's to cut all this fresh air and sea breezes," she said. "Too corny." She sat up again.

"When I met him at the White Hound, when I blew my cover, do you remember, I wrote to you?" she asked him. Geraint nodded. "He told me the story was public knowledge."

"Marina didn't seem to know anything about it," Geraint said. "That's strange, isn't it?"

"Hang on, don't confuse me," she said. "It may be public knowledge that the Morton sister went missing. But nobody knew what happened next. The thing that Roddy is so pleased about must be some further twist in the story, the little weasel. There's some gobbet of scandal that he's found from poking about, squalid little bugger. That's the thing he lifts the cloth off when he's alone in his room, that's the thing he's holding over Marina."

"He's made a big impression on you, hasn't he?" Geraint said.

"Seriously," Janice said. "He's got some sort of blackmail in mind, maybe not crudely, for money, but he thinks he knows something that gives him a hold on Marina, or her mother." She stubbed her cigarette out on the Saint's chair, grinding ash into the delicate spirals of lichen. "There's something more. We haven't cracked it."

Geraint sat up. To their left a little stunted pine was growing on the lip of the cliff. On the margin of sky and sea a tanker was slipping out of sight. He felt the faint pressure of Janice's shoulder as she leaned against him.

"We think the past is fixed," he said. "But it's not, it's fluid. It's constantly altered by what happens next, it never stays the same. We can't get any comfort from our memories, because they're playing over a surface that's moving all the time. The meaning of what we remember keeps changing." Janice looked at him.

"In that case we have no idea of what's happening in the present either," she said. "What we're doing at this moment, sitting here on this cliff-top, what this means, will only be revealed in the future. Anyway, listen, I'm hungry." Geraint felt the shift of muscle in her upper arm against his.

"I already thought of that," he said. "I'm taking you out to lunch."

"Taking me out to lunch?" Janice said. "Does that mean we're on a date?"

"Time will tell," he said. "How's Geraint, by the way?"

"He's getting free," she said. "He's still pursuing the same obsessive little itineraries: visit the Gallery, explore the town, eat bratwurst and rösti, nod and smile at Frau Henker and Fraulein Trost, but he can feel the oppressive weight lifting, beginning to lighten."

"Can he tell the sisters apart now?"

"Yes he can, and he recognises that's a good sign, he's beginning to connect to the world again."

"So how does he tell?"

"They look quite different, it's just he could never remember which name to attach to which. Fraulein Trost is the older one, with the mole." She put a hand out to steady herself as the car bumped and swayed down the track. "The best thing is, he never sees the Grey Goose again, although of course he doesn't know that yet. But time goes by and there's no sign of him, and it begins to seem to Geraint that all that predatory power, all that fire behind the eyes, was an illusion, that it had shattered from the impact of a single decisive act. Sometimes he wonders if the American was a hallucination, a sort of Golem that he had conjured up from inside himself. But that's frightening; he doesn't like to think he may have been that delusional. So far he hasn't dared ask the sisters where the American went, in case they give him a blank, concerned: *what American?* look. Also, he doesn't think his German is up to it."

The bells of St Michael's were ringing as people came out of church. In the Square, swallows were diving and banking through the arches of the old market building.

"I booked a table at that new place," Geraint said. "Hwyel said it was good."

"The Fig Leaf," Janice said.

"The Vine Leaf, you idiot," Geraint said, laughing.

They'd spent a lot of money on the place. A revolving glass door opened into a bar area that took up most of the ground floor. Enormous mirrors fragmented and replicated space into disjointed perspectives. Janice whistled.

"Impressed," she said.

The whole of the end wall was taken up by the bar. There was a young man sitting with his back to them on one of the bar stools. As they crossed the room, Janice lengthened her stride and swung herself up onto the stool beside him.

"Roddy," she said. "Look at you!" Geraint climbed onto the stool on Roddy's right. The boy hunched, pulling his shoulders in. "Don't look so hunted. We're not trying to corner you." Roddy was wearing a pale linen jacket and a bright yellow shirt. He straightened his shoulders. Janice stroked the sleeve of his jacket. "Who's been giving you fashion tips, Roddy?" He blushed, frowning. "Doesn't he look great?"

"Elegant," Geraint said. "Let me buy you a drink, Roddy."

"How's journalism?" Janice asked him. "How are your investigations going?" Roddy glanced at his watch, then at the revolving doors reflected in the mirrors behind the bar. "How's the missing sister?" He shrugged. "Have you found her yet?" Roddy sipped at a glass of wine.

"Anything's possible," he said.

"I had you down as a pint man," Janice said. "I suppose Rioja is part of the make-over."

"And why are you both so interested?" Roddy said. "What's your problem?"

"If you've found the missing sister you have a responsibility to let the family know," Geraint said. "And I don't think you've done that yet, have you?"

"That's what we're interested in," Janice said. "What exactly are you up to?"

"Let's just get this straight," Roddy said. "You don't know if I've located Marina's aunt, and you don't know if I've told her, or her mother." His eyes flicked from his watch to the mirrors behind the bar again.

"I think you've been stood up, Roddy," Janice told him.

"You don't know much, in fact," Roddy said.

"I think you could get yourself into a lot of trouble," Geraint said.

Roddy stood up. "Thanks for the drink," he said. He straightened his jacket, patting and smoothing the material.

"Have you ever considered a career in modelling?" Janice asked him. She watched him as he left the room, shaking her head. "That felt like round two to Roddy," she said. "A bit bruising."

"I'll have to talk to Rosie properly," Geraint said. "She gets so agitated though, you feel you could do a lot of harm. And my mother's so confused." He sighed.

"Let's go and eat," Janice said. "I'm starving."

* * *

Geraint hung the chart on the school-room wall behind the teacher's desk: *British Butterflies*. Time had dulled the insects' colours to a moth-like, autumnal uniformity of brown and grey. He looked round the room. They still had to decide what to do about the classroom clock. Mike wanted it repaired or the movement replaced so it would keep time; the idea of time standing still depressed him, he said. The audio loop was running, the teacher asking a question, a piping babel of suggestions from the class. The Assize Court audio was running next door, the two scenarios blending in a weird dissonant counterpoint:

> *Tomos Williams, the Court has heard that on the fourteenth of April you and a companion...* Fi Miss! Gofyn fi! Da iawn, Beti!

The lights were off in the Early Christian Monuments room; the stones slouched in the dim light. Geraint flicked the overhead spotlights on and the shapes came to life, scored with circles, crosses, incised Latin inscriptions. *Rufinus* he read, *the devoted champion of righteousness.* If the attribution was good, Rufinus was St Brygga's contemporary. They might have met, although Briggana would have been a young girl when the holy man died. She might have seen this stone. Geraint thought of the arc of her life, stranger than a rainbow, which ended with her name carved in marble in Ancient Corinth, famous for her piety, revered as a worker of miracles, the faithful servant of the Emperor Justinian.

The Eastern Empire was a world built out of words, Geraint thought, from the Word itself, the Logos, to its infinitely numerous manifestations: inscriptions, prayers, proclamations, liturgies. Justinian's Code of Civil Law was a million words long. In this world of text, perhaps it wasn't surprising that Briggana's name had survived. Rufinus had been luckier to be remembered as an individual, not to be swept away. His name, and a few words of acclamation, were fixed points in a landscape where so much was conjectural, persisting only in folklore and incoherent tradition. If St Brygga had come back, he thought, if the pilgrimage of her life had eventually returned her to her birthplace in the West, no faint testimony, notched in Ogham or scratched in Latin might ever be found. Nothing beyond the bulk of the stone on the headland. Thinking about the Chair, Geraint felt something tighten in his chest, as though his heart had made a fist.

Janice was in her workshop on the top floor. She was wearing goggles, and was playing the flame of a blow-torch over a twisted piece of metal on the bench.

"I found her," Geraint said. "St Brygga came back to Wales. I followed her all the way to Corinth, and now I realise I followed her all the way back."

Janice switched the torch off and pushed her goggles up her forehead.

"I don't understand why I didn't see it before," Geraint said.

"What have you found?" she asked him.

"It was there all the time," he said. "St Brygga's Chair. The Chair proves she came back." Janice swung herself up onto the workbench and watched him, swinging her legs. "The question you have to ask yourself is: why is it called St Brygga's Chair?" Geraint said. "We don't think about it because it comes from somewhere so far back in time that it's taken for granted. It's like a place-name, as though it was topographical, like a mountain or a lake."

"It's called St Brygga's Chair because it's associated with her. She was born here. I'm missing something, aren't I?"

"It's easy to do," Geraint said. "Most of what we know about her comes from that Life of Eugenius. That stuff about renouncing their patrimony and going to Armorica. Do you remember? St Eugenius goes blind, Briggana gets summoned by the white hound, she sets off to Rome." Janice nodded, her eyes following him as he paced the room. "When they leave Wales for Brittany, she's a young girl, nothing special about her, except that she happens to be the sister of a saint. Why would that stone on the headland be named after her? Nobody in Wales knew who she was." He looked at Janice. "She became consecrated to God, canonised as a saint, famous for working miracles, all of this on the other side of the world. People who knew her here would have seen her set off on a journey, and never come back, just a girl who disappeared. Why would they have named the Chair after her if she never came back? She must have come back." He walked over to the window and looked out. A school mini-bus drew in to the car-park: Ysgol Dewi Sant. "Damn, I forgot all about that," he said. "I'm giving them a talk and a guided tour. They're early." He turned back to Janice. "Do you see? She will have felt the pilgrimage wasn't complete until she returned. She will have come back: old, sunburned, famous, surrounded by exotic followers."

"Like someone out of *OK Magazine,*" Janice said.

"Listen," he said, laughing. "She comes back with an aura, ten times stronger than fame, flowing out of her, the sacred light pouring out in all directions. She is an aspect of the Godhead. The sacred is magically present in her world, it acts directly on reality. Everything she touches is sanctified, everything become possible. She walks up to the headland, completing the last few steps of the circle of her journey. When she sits down on the stone, it's transformed, it becomes hers." He walked to the door. Janice smiled at him.

"It's good to see you so happy," she said. She sat very still, watching the door swing slowly shut behind him, hearing the clatter of his footsteps on the stairs.

★ ★ ★

They got the school-room finished on time, Mike insisting on an awkward little ceremony, a dedication, he said, to the belief that the past was a living thing. Standing behind the teacher's desk, under the faded butterflies, he congratulated them on their efforts. Geraint drank the little glass of cheap sherry, realising that he hadn't called in on his mother since the beginning of the week, noting with a sudden anxiety that with Aled not visiting he needed to drop round more often.

She was watching the news. He made a pot of tea while she called through to him in the kitchen from her armchair. She looked tired.

"There's a tin of biscuits there," she said. "Beti brought them round. She knows I don't like them. I was going to give them to Rosie, for the journey, but she wouldn't take them."

"When did Rosie leave?" Geraint asked.

"Not long," his mother said. "I told her to stay and get her strength, but she wouldn't. You know how she is." His mother smiled to herself, shaking her head. "She said this was an important journey, a special one. I said: *You always say that Rosie* but she said no, not like this."

Geraint sat in the other armchair, facing her across the television.

"How long have you known Rosie?" he asked. "How did you get to know her?"

"Turn that thing off, won't you, Geraint?" she said. "It's too gloomy, and I've lost the what-do-you-call."

"Remote," Geraint said. He leaned across and pushed the button, the set shutting down with a little squeak. He looked at her, waiting for her to answer. She shut her eyes.

"It's nice of you to call," she said. "I never see Aled these days. Just Beti and her biscuits." She snorted with laughter. "Which she knows I won't eat. Why does she do it?"

"How did you get to know Rosie, Mother?" he asked again. "Where's she from, in the first place?"

His mother opened her eyes.

"She's from here of course," she said. "She won't talk about the past though, quite right. She won't discuss the past."

"That's fine," Geraint said. "But she's not here now. There's something I'd really like to clear up."

His mother stared at him.

"You can't expect me to talk behind her back," she said. "Rosie knows I wouldn't do that, she trusts me." There was a silence. "Would you turn the television on, Geraint?" his mother said. "I want to watch the news, I've lost the what-do-you-call."

"Remote," Geraint said.

"Remote," his mother said. "Why can I never remember that word?"

★ ★ ★

188

On Friday he had an email from the Corinth Department of Antiquities:

We ought to inform you that until the present day the location of the Sanctuary of Necessity and Violence referred by Pausanias [2.1.1-5.1] has not been authoritatively established. Thank you for your kind enquiry.

He leaned back in his chair, picturing the sudden rise of sheer granite, glowing like heated steel. Another email came in. He leaned forward and clicked it open.

Dear Dad, I'm working at a sailing school near Kalamata – I'm an instructor! I told them I'd been sailing all my life, the first couple of times I took the boat out was a pretty steep learning curve, I can tell you. I'll stay here until the end of the summer, don't know after that. I'm not sure if there's a way back from here, maybe I'll just keep sailing. Don't worry about me ☺ Aled

He rang Elaine.

"I know," she said. "I heard from him this morning. Hang on, I'm just getting in a cab." He heard her murmur something over the idling rattle of the engine and the tinny thump of the door. "Sloane Square," she said. "That's better, what were you saying?" She must have pulled the window down; Geraint could hear the rush of air, and the far-away whooping of a police siren. "I know, it's ridiculous," she said. "Why don't you cut through Draycott Avenue? What were you saying, Geraint? Have you written back to him?"

"Not yet," Geraint said. "I only just got his email."

"Mine was pretty short and sweet," Elaine said. He heard the snap of her cigarette lighter, and a long, sighing breath. "But it was wonderful to hear from him," she said. "Just wonderful."

He showed the email to Janice.

"I'll buy you a drink after work tonight," she said. "We'll go the the Fig Leaf and I'll buy you champagne."

"The Vine Leaf," Geraint said. "You idiot."

They sat at a marble-topped table in a recessed area of the wine bar, the mirrored walls on either side of them replicating their image over and over in a curving regression, like playing cards fanned out on a table.

Janice raised her glass, the mirrors picking the movement up in shimmering arpeggios of repetition. "Here's to Aled," she said. "And to you."

"To Aled," Geraint said. "The sailing instructor."

"The pilgrim," Janice said. "To Aled, the pilgrim. To the new Aled, whoever he turns out to be." She set her glass down on the table. "You have to let the old Aled go," she said. "Don't get trapped." She looked around the room. "Makes a change from the Bull," she said.

"The Bull isn't really big on champagne," Geraint said.

"I like it here," Janice said. "It could be anywhere. It could be Rotterdam, it could be Munich."

"I like it here too," he said, touching her glass with his. "Munich as in your book?" Janice nodded.

"I wanted to tell you, things have been getting better for Geraint," she said.

"Tell me."

"He's getting ready to return," Janice said. "He's been taking enormously long walks around the city, walking all day, trying to make sense of the strange journey he's been on, but he knows that soon he'll make a final visit to the Gallery to say goodbye to Salomé; he'll settle up with Fraulein Trost and Frau Henker; they'll take a long time making up his bill, and they both have tears in their eyes. He knows it's time to go home."

"What sort of home-life has he got?" Geraint asked. "Is he married?"

"Divorced."

"Has he got a girlfriend?"

"I'm not sure if he has," Janice said. She looked at him, her smile deepening. "I'll have to do something about that."

The bar became musical with conversation, the click and chink of glass on marble.

"Marina!" Janice called out, raising her hand. "Marina!" The girl saw them and smiled, moving through the crowd towards them. "Come and sit with us," Janice said. "You look fantastic, you can

190

sprinkle a little glamour on us." Geraint fetched another glass.

"What are you celebrating?" Marina asked.

"We're not quite sure yet," Janice said, glancing at Geraint with a quick smile. "Have you had any more trouble from Roddy?"

"Trouble?" Marina said. "No, he's been amazing."

"Amazing?" Janice said, clicking her glass against Marina's. "What form does that take?"

Marina's face seemed to clear and soften, as though a hand had stroked her forehead, her eyes shining. "Of course," she said. "You don't know what's been happening, do you? Roddy said he'd seen the two of you, but you hadn't talked properly." Geraint and Janice glanced at each other.

"Properly?" Geraint said.

"I haven't see you since that time you came to Morton, have I?" Marina said. She shook her head. "I was completely wrong about it all." She glanced round at the doors as people came in. "You remember the photograph album?"

Janice nodded.

"Do you remember the pictures of the two girls?"

"Of course," Geraint said.

"One of them was my mother," Marina said. "Did you know the other one was my aunt?" She raised her voice, a sharp note of anger ringing in it.

"Did you know I even had an aunt?" She glared at them for a moment, then grinned suddenly. "Don't look so worried," she said. "I'm not cross with you."

"Roddy said something about it," Janice said hesitantly, "a while ago."

Marina nodded, finishing the wine in her glass.

"Apparently lots of people knew," she said. "Except me. It seems my mother forgot to mention it to me."

"He came to see us in the Museum," Geraint said. "We thought he was trying to make trouble."

"So I never knew she had a sister," Marina said. "A sister who disappeared."

"Maybe she thought it would upset you," Janice said. "When you were little."

"Roddy wasn't making trouble," Marina said. "The opposite, in fact."

"Have you talked to your mother about it?" Geraint asked. "I'm sure she thought there were good reasons for not telling you."

"What's the opposite of trouble?" Janice asked.

"That's not the biggest problem," Marina said. "Her not telling me. That's not what finished me off. I'm leaving home, by the way, did I tell you? But that's not really the reason." A group of young men were pushing through the revolving doors in a mock scuffle. Marina looked round, scanning their faces quickly. "Roddy found her; didn't he tell you about this?"

"Why are you leaving home? Janice asked.

"It's not so much Roddy found her," Marina said. "More like he found out about her. I thought you knew this. He told my mother he was doing a story about Morton House, the family history, all that stuff. Mother must have thought he knew all about her little secret, she lost her temper, shouted the whole thing out at him." She looked at them, shaking her head, her eyes narrowed. "*Bag lady! Crazy tramp!* That's what she said. *I won't have her here!* Can you imagine? She's known for ages. Rosemary came back a long time ago, my mother wouldn't have her in the house, she chased her away." Janice and Geraint stared at her. "Rosemary's quite confused. She's had a terrible life, it's like she's terrified of mother, she just wandered away again."

"Do you know where Rosie is now?" Geraint asked. "Rosemary?"

"She's at Morton," Marina said. "Mother's had a change of heart, with a little help from me. I never thought I'd dare talk to my mother like that, but she knew what a dreadful thing she'd done. So, she's going to look after her, get her some help. Maybe it'll all work out now." She shook her head. "I'm still leaving though. I can't really forgive her. Anyway, I need to get away, for a while at least."

Looking up, Geraint saw Roddy pushing his way towards them, the same linen jacket, an even brighter shirt.

"Look who's here," he said. "It's the fearless reporter." As he spoke, he saw the smile that illuminated Marina, lighting her up with

192

a brilliance that the mirrors replicated. Roddy came over to their table and stood beside her. She reached her arm around him, stroking the small of his back. He leaned down and kissed the top of her head.

"Roddy's taking some time out," she said. "We're going travelling. I want him to see Greece, so we'll probably start there, see what happens after that."

Roddy pulled up a chair and sat down next to Marina, nodding to Geraint and Janice.

"Greece!" Janice said. "Send us a postcard, won't you." She lit a cigarette, flapping the smoke away. "Keep in touch," she said, "Don't just disappear."

"Didn't I hear Aled was in Greece?" Marina said to Geraint. "I haven't seen him for ages. What's he been up to?"

"We should get going," Roddy said. "Goodbye, you two."

★ ★ ★

At the bottom of the Graig Goch track a pheasant was admiring his reflection in the roadside mirror, turning his head from one side to the other as though finding his best profile. He glanced absent-mindedly at Geraint as the car passed him, then turned back to peer into the mirror, striking a new pose.

The phone had rung for a long time at Morton House before Marina's mother answered it. Geraint imagined it ringing somewhere in one of those unwelcoming rooms. Mrs Price-Ellis had sounded distracted; it had taken him several attempts before she took in what he was phoning about.

"And you want to bring it here?" she had said finally.

"No one at Blaenteg seems to know how it fetched up there," he had told her. "It seems to me it ought to come back to Morton House."

"And there are pictures of the family in it?" she said, sounding outraged. "Pictures of me? And you had it at the Museum?"

He parked on the north side of the house, the car tyres creaking on the gravel. He picked up the photograph album, brushing cigarette ash off the scuffed leather cover, smiling to himself, seeing Janice for a moment. Beyond the house, the parkland sloped away to the south, towards the headland and the sea. In front of him a shallow flight of steps led up into the formal gardens, geometric flowerbeds set in rigid arrangements of granite terracing and squares of lawn. In the centre, a small fountain dribbled water into a marble bowl.

He started across the terrace. As he turned at the corner of the house, he became aware of two women standing together in front of a stunted rose-bush. They turned towards him as he approached. They stood awkwardly close together, side by side, one a head taller than the other, scowling as if at a camera or perhaps squinting in the watery sunlight.

"Good morning," Geraint said, nodding to Marina's mother. "Good morning Rosie. My mother's been wondering where you were."

"I'm here," Rosie said with her sweet, sudden smile. "Tell her I'm here."

Geraint found himself listening to the feeble dribble of the fountain. The plants in the flowerbeds had an exhausted look, as though the soil was dying. Meanwhile, he thought, in Liminidhi, the never-failing stream is trickling under the road and out onto the bright shingle. Swallows are flashing among the cypress trees and ruined colonnades, and the roadsides are sticky with fallen figs. On the headland across the bay, in the twilight, the lighthouse opens its pale eye, looks away.

Many thanks to my peerless travelling companion, Edward Bates; the wonderful people at the National Missing Persons Helpline; Gwen Davies of Alcemi; Dyfed-Powys Police; the criminal investigation division of Corinth police force; the British Consulate at Athens, and Academi for a writer's bursary. Love and thanks to Ruth, Tom and Elin, and many others for support and inspiration.

ALCEMI

voices

fiction

stories

contemporary

new

authentic

vulnerable

diverse

international

original

ironic

'Offbeat, subtle, haunting, fresh.'
Kate Long

SALVAGE

Gee Williams

ALCEMI

A sophisticated thriller ranging between Wales, north-west England
and Goa, which explores possession, betrayal and how much we can
afford to lose.

£9.99
ISBN: 978-0-9555272-0-3

ALCEMI

www.alcemi.eu

Talybont Ceredigion Cymru SY24 5AP
e-mail gwen@ylolfa.com
phone (01970) 832 304
fax 832 782